O...
Moss-Green Eyes And Her Body Had Gone Soft And Pliant.

Spending a short amount of time with Marcus while she'd shown him around the bakery had been…not horrible. If it hadn't been for the secret Vanessa was hiding just one floor above, she might even have gotten him that cup of coffee and invited him to stay a while longer.

Which was a really bad idea, so it was better that he'd taken off when he had.

She had Danny pressed to her chest, content now that his belly was being filled, when she heard footsteps coming up the stairs. There was no time to jump up and hide the baby, no time to yell for Aunt Helen to run interference. One minute she was glancing around for a blanket to cover her exposed chest, and the next she was frozen in place, staring with alarm at her stunned but furious ex-husband.

Dear Reader,

I had such a good time with *Her Little Secret, His Hidden Heir,* especially since Marc and Vanessa's story is set mainly in a bakery. Writing about all the delicious goodies Vanessa and her aunt were baking up made me hungry for every single one.

So I thought it might be fun to share one of those very special recipes with you. (It's one of my personal favorites.) Turn to page six for details. And if you get the chance to try it, please drop me a line to let me know what you think!

I hope you enjoy Marc and Vanessa's story and the cookies! They're excellent with a glass of cold milk, by the way.

All my best,

Heidi Betts
www.HeidiBetts.com

HEIDI BETTS

HER LITTLE SECRET, HIS HIDDEN HEIR

For my wonderful new Desire editor, Charles Griemsman. It's been a delight working with and getting to know you this past year, and I'm looking forward to sharing many more *Desire*-able moments in the future.

ISBN-13: 978-0-373-73104-6

HER LITTLE SECRET, HIS HIDDEN HEIR

Recycling programs for this product may not exist in your area.

www.Harlequin.com

Printed in U.S.A.

Books by Heidi Betts

Desire

HEIDI BETTS

An avid romance reader since junior high, national bestselling author Heidi Betts knew early on that she wanted to write these wonderful stories of love and adventure. It wasn't until her freshman year of college, however, when she spent the entire night before finals reading a romance novel instead of studying, that she decided to take the road less traveled and follow her dream.

Soon after joining Romance Writers of America, Heidi's writing began to garner attention, including placing in the esteemed Golden Heart competition three years in a row. The recipient of numerous awards and stellar reviews, Heidi's books combine believable characters with compelling plotlines, and are consistently described as "delightful," "sizzling" and "wonderfully witty."

For news, fun and information about upcoming books, be sure to visit Heidi online at HeidiBetts.com.

CHOCOLATE PEANUT BUTTER PINWHEELS

INGREDIENTS:
1 cup butter, softened
1 cup light brown sugar, firmly packed
1 cup peanut butter (you can add more if you like
your cookies really peanut buttery)
1 egg
1 teaspoon vanilla extract
2 cups flour
1 teaspoon baking soda
½ teaspoon salt

INGREDIENTS FOR FILLING:
2 cups (or one 12-ounce bag) chocolate chips
2 tablespoons butter

DIRECTIONS:

1. In large bowl, cream butter and sugar until light and fluffy.

2. Add peanut butter, egg and vanilla. Beat until smooth.

3. Add flour, baking soda and salt and mix until dough is formed. Cover and refrigerate for 30 minutes.

4. Make filling by melting chocolate chips and butter together in a slow cooker on lowest setting or in a double boiler.

5. Remove dough from refrigerator. Roll half of it into an 11 x 17 inch rectangle on a lightly floured surface.

6. Spread half of chocolate filling evenly over dough.

7. Roll tightly from long side. Wrap in plastic wrap. Refrigerate until firm—at least 8 hours or overnight.

8. Repeat with remaining dough and filling.

9. Cut into 1/8-inch slices and bake in 325°F oven for about 8 minutes or until lightly browned.

10. Remove to wire racks to cool.

Prologue

Vanessa Keller—soon to be simply Vanessa Mason again—sat at the foot of her hotel-room bed, staring at the small plastic wand in her hand. She blinked, feeling her heart pound, her stomach roll and her vision go fuzzy around the edges.

As bad luck went, this ranked right up there with having your plane go down on the way to your honeymoon destination or getting hit by a bus right after you'd won the million-dollar lotto.

And the irony of the situation…

A harsh laugh escaped her lungs, taking with it a puff of the stale air she'd been holding onto for the past several minutes.

She was newly divorced from a husband she'd *thought* was the man of her dreams, staying in a downtown Pittsburgh hotel because she didn't know quite what to do with her life now that the rug had been yanked out from under her. And if that wasn't enough to make her wonder where things had gone so wrong, now she was pregnant.

Pregnant. With her ex-husband's child, when she hadn't managed to conceive in the three years they'd been married, even though they'd tried...or at least hadn't worked to prevent it.

What in heaven's name was she going to do?

Pushing to her feet on less-than-steady legs, she crossed to the wide desk against the far wall and dropped into its cushioned chair. Her hands shook as she laid the small plastic stick on the flat surface and dragged the phone closer.

Taking deep, shuddering breaths, she told herself she could do this. Told herself it was the right thing to do, and however he reacted, she would handle it.

This was not a bid to get back together. Vanessa wasn't sure she would want to, even with a baby now in the picture. But he deserved to know he was going to be a father, regardless of the current state of their relationship.

With cold fingers, she dialed the familiar number, knowing his assistant would answer. She'd never cared for Trevor Storch; he was a weaselly little brownnoser, treating her more as an annoyance than as the wife of the CEO of a multimillion-dollar company and *his boss.*

After only one ring, Trevor's squeaky, singsong voice came on the line. "Keller Corporation, Marcus Keller's office. How may I help you?"

"It's Vanessa," she said without preamble—he knew full well who she was. He was probably privy to more of the details about her marriage and subsequent divorce than he deserved to be, too. "I need to talk to Marc."

"I'm sorry, Miss Mason, Mr. Keller isn't available."

His use of her maiden name—not to mention calling her *Miss*—struck Vanessa's heart like the tip of a knife. No doubt he'd done it deliberately.

"It's important," she said, not bothering to correct or argue with him. She'd done enough of that in the past, as well as overlooking his snide attitude just to keep the peace; she didn't have to do it anymore, either.

"I'm sorry," he told her again, "but Mr. Keller has instructed me to tell you that there's nothing you could possibly have to say to him that he wants to hear. Good day."

And with that, the line went dead, leaving Vanessa open-mouthed with shock. If hearing herself called "Miss Mason" rather than "Mrs. Keller" felt like a knife tip being inserted into her heart, then being told her ex-husband wouldn't even deign to speak with her any longer thrust the blade the rest of the way in to the hilt and twisted it sharply.

She'd known Marc was angry with her, knew they'd parted on less than friendly terms. But never in a million years would she have expected him to cut her off so callously.

He'd loved her once, hadn't he? She'd certainly loved him. And yet they'd come to this—virtual strangers who couldn't even speak a civil word to one another.

But that answered the question of what she was going to do. She was going to be a single mother, and without Marcus's money and support—which she wouldn't have taken, with or without the prenup—she'd better find a way to take care of herself and the baby—and she'd better do it fast.

One

One year later...

Marcus Keller flexed his fingers on the warm leather of the steering wheel, his sleek black Mercedes hugging the road as he took the narrow curves leading into Summerville faster than was probably wise.

The small Pennsylvania town was only three hours from his own home in Pittsburgh, but it might as well have been a world away. Where Pittsburgh was ninety percent concrete and city lights, Summerville was thick forests, green grass, quaint houses and a small downtown area that reminded Marcus of a modern version of Mayberry.

He slowed his speed, taking the time to examine the storefronts as he passed. A drug store, a post office, a bar and grill, a gift shop...and a bakery.

Lifting his foot from the gas, he slowed even more, studying the bright yellow awning and fancy black lettering declaring it to be The Sugar Shack…the red neon sign in the window letting customers know they were open…and the handful of people inside, enjoying freshly made baked goods.

It looked inviting, which was important in the food service industry. He was tempted to lower his window and see if he could actually smell the delicious scents of breads and cookies and pies in the air.

But there was more to running a successful business than a cute name and an attractive front window, and if he was going to put money into The Sugar Shack, he wanted to know it was a sound investment.

At the corner, he took a left and continued down a side street, following the directions he'd been given to reach the offices of Blake and Fetzer, Financial Advisors. He'd worked with Brian Blake before, though never on an investment this far from home or this close to Blake's own offices. Still, the man had never steered him wrong, which made Marcus more willing to take time off work and make the long drive.

A few blocks down the street, he noticed a lone woman walking quickly on three-inch heels. Given the uneven pavement and pebbles littering the sidewalk, she wasn't having an easy time of it. She also seemed distracted, rooting around inside an oversize handbag rather than keeping her attention on where she was going.

A niggle of something uncomfortable skated through his belly. She reminded him somehow of his ex-wife. A bit heavier and curvier, her coppery hair cut short instead of left to flow halfway down her back, but still very similar. Especially the way she walked and dressed. This woman was wearing a white blouse and a black skirt with a short slit at the back, framing a pair of long, lovely legs. No jacket and no clunky accessories, which followed Vanessa's personal style to a T.

Shifting his gaze back to the road, he tamped down on

whatever emotion had his chest going tight. Guilt? Regret? Simple sentimentality? He wasn't sure and didn't care to examine the unexpected feelings too closely.

They'd been divorced for over a year. Better to put it all behind him and move on, as he was sure Vanessa had done.

Spotting the offices of Blake and Fetzer, he pulled into the diminutive three-car lot at the back of the building, cut the engine and stepped out into the warm spring day. With any luck, this meeting and the subsequent tour of The Sugar Shack would only take a couple of hours, then he could be back on the road and headed home. Small town life might be fine for some people, but Marcus would be only too happy to get back to the hustle and bustle of the city and the life he'd made for himself there.

Vanessa stopped outside Brian Blake's office, taking a moment to straighten her blouse and skirt, run a hand through her short-cropped hair and touch up her lipstick. It had been a long time since she'd gotten this dressed up and she was sorely out of practice.

It didn't help, either, that all of the nicer clothes she'd acquired while being married to Marcus were now at least one size too small. That meant her top was a bit too snug across the chest, her skirt was a good inch shorter than she would have liked and darned if the waistband wasn't cutting off her circulation.

Thankfully, the town of Summerville didn't require her to dress up this much, even for Sunday services. Otherwise, she may have had to invest in a new wardrobe, and given what a hard time she was having just keeping her head above water and her business afloat, that was an added expense she definitely could not afford.

Deciding that her appearance was about as good as it was going to get at this late date, she took a deep breath and pushed through the door. Blake and Fetzer's lone receptionist greeted her with a wide smile, informed her that Brian and the potential investor were waiting in his office, and told her to go right in.

She took another steadying breath and before stepping inside sent a quick prayer heavenward that the wealthy entrepreneur Brian had found to hopefully invest in her fledging enterprise would find The Sugar Shack worthy of his financial backing.

The first thing she saw was Brian sitting behind his desk, smiling as he chatted with the visitor facing away from her in one of the guest chairs. The man had dark hair that barely dusted the collar of his charcoal-gray jacket and was tapping a tan, long-fingered hand on the arm of his chair, as though he was impatient to get down to business.

As soon as Brian spotted her, his smile widened and he rose to his feet. "Vanessa," he greeted her, "you're right on time. Allow me to introduce you to the man I *hope* will become an investor in your wonderful bakery. Marcus Keller, this is Vanessa Mason. Vanessa this is—"

"We've met."

Marcus's voice hit her like a sledgehammer to the solar plexus, but it was only one of a series of rapid-fire shocks to her system. Brian had spoken her ex-husband's name and her stomach had plummeted all the way to her feet. At the same time, Marcus had risen from his seat and turned to face her, and her heart had started to pound against her rib cage like a runaway freight train.

She saw him standing in front of her, black hair glinting midnight blue in the dappled sunlight streaming through the tall, multipaned windows lining one wall of the office, his green eyes gleaming with devilment. Yet his suit-and-tie image wavered and no amount of blinking brought him into focus.

"Hello, Vanessa," he murmured softly.

Brushing his jacket aside, he slipped his hands into the front pockets of his matching charcoal slacks, adopting a negligent pose. He looked so comfortable and amused, while she felt as though an army of ants was crawling beneath her skin.

How in God's name could this have happened? How could she not know that *he* was the potential investor? How could Brian not realize that Marcus was her *ex*-husband?

She wanted to kick herself for not asking more questions or insisting on being given more details about today's meeting. But then, she hadn't really cared who Brian's mystery investor was, had she? She'd cared only that he was rich and seemed willing to partner up with small business owners in the hopes of a big payoff down the road.

She'd convinced herself she was desperate and needed a quick influx of cash to keep The Sugar Shack's doors open. But she would *never* be desperate enough to take charity from the man who had broken her heart and turned his back on her when she'd needed him the most.

Not bothering to address Marcus, she turned her gaze to Brian. "I'm sorry, but this isn't going to work out," she told him, then promptly turned on her heel and marched back out of the office building.

She was down the front steps and halfway up the block before she heard the first call.

"Vanessa! Vanessa, wait!"

The three-inch pumps she'd worn because they went so well with her outfit—and because she'd wanted to make a good impression—pinched her toes as she nearly ran the length of the uneven sidewalk in the direction of The Sugar Shack. All she wanted was to get away from Marcus, away from those glittering eyes and the arrogant tilt of his chin.

She didn't care that he was yelling for her, or that she could hear his footsteps keeping pace several yards behind her.

"Vanessa!"

Turning the corner only a short distance from The Sugar Shack, her steps faltered. Her heart lurched and her blood chilled.

Oh, no. She'd been so angry, so eager to get away from her ex-husband and escape back to the safety of the bakery that she'd forgotten that's where Danny was. And if there was anything she needed to protect more than her own sanity, it was her son.

Suddenly, she couldn't take another step, coming to a jerky stop only feet from the bakery door. Marcus rounded the corner a moment later, coming to an equally abrupt halt when he spotted her simply standing there like a panicked and disheveled department store mannequin.

He was slightly out of breath, and she found that more than a little satisfying. It was a nice change from his normal state of being calm, cool and always in control. And nothing less than he deserved, given what he was putting her through now.

"Finally," he muttered, sounding completely put out. "Why did you run?" He wanted to know. "We may be divorced, but that doesn't mean we can't sit and have a civil conversation."

"I have nothing to say to you," she bit out. *And there was nothing she had to say that he wanted to hear.* The cruel declaration replayed through her mind, bringing with it a fresh stab of pain and reminding her of just how important it was to keep him away from her child.

"What about this business of yours?" he asked, running a hand through his thick, dark hair before smoothing his tie and buttoning his suit jacket, once again the epitome of entrepreneurial precision. "It sounds like you could use the capital and I'm always on the lookout for a good investment."

"I don't want your money," she told him.

He inclined his head, acknowledging the sincerity of her words. "But do you need it?"

He asked the question in a low tone, with no hint of condescension and not as though he meant to dangle his wealth over her head like a plump, juicy carrot. Instead, he sounded willing to help her if she needed it.

Oh, she needed help, but not of the strings-attached variety. And not from her cold, unfeeling ex-husband.

Fighting the urge to grab whatever money he was willing to toss her way and run, she straightened her spine, squared her shoulders and reminded herself that she was doing just fine on her own. She didn't need a man—any man—to ride in and rescue her.

"The bakery is doing quite well, thank you," she replied, her voice clipped. "And even if it weren't, I wouldn't need anything from you."

Marc opened his mouth, about to reply and possibly try to change her mind, when Brian Blake rushed around the corner. He skidded to a jerky halt when he saw them, looking frazzled and alarmed. For a second, he stood there, breathing heavily, his gaze darting back and forth between the two of them. Then he shook his head and his puzzlement seemed to clear.

"Mr. Keller...Vanessa..." He took another moment to suck in much-needed oxygen, his Adam's apple riding up and down above the tight collar of his pale blue dress shirt. "This isn't at all how I'd planned for this meeting to go," he told them apologetically. "If you'll just come back to the office.... Let's sit down and see if we can't work something out."

A touch of guilt tugged at Vanessa's chest. Brian was a good guy. He didn't deserve to suffer or be put in the middle

of an acrimonious situation just because she despised Marc
and refused to have anything more to do with him—let alone
go into business with him.

"I'm sorry, Brian," she apologized. "I appreciate everything
you've done for me, but this particular partnership just isn't
going to work."

For a minute, Brian looked as though he meant to argue.
Noting the firm expression on her face, however, he released
a sigh of resignation and nodded. "I understand."

"Actually," Marc said, "I'm still very much interested in
hearing about the bakery."

Brian's eyes widened with a spark of relief, but Vanessa
immediately tensed.

"No, Marcus," she told him, her firm tone brooking no
arguments. Not that that had ever stopped him before.

"It sounds like it might be a sound investment, *Nessa*,"
he retorted, arching a single dark brow and using his old pet
name for her. No doubt to put her off balance. "I drove three
hours to get here and I'd prefer not to turn right around and
go back empty-handed." He paused for a beat, letting that sink
in. Then he added, "At least give me a tour."

No. Oh, no. She definitely couldn't let him into the bakery.
That would be even more dangerous than simply having him
in town, aware that she lived here now, as well.

She opened her mouth to say so, linking her arms across
her chest to let him know she had no intention of changing
her mind, when Brian stopped her. Touching her shoulder, he
tipped his head, signaling her to follow him a few steps away,
out of earshot of Marcus.

"Miss Mason. Vanessa," he said, dropping formalities.
"Think about this. Please. I know Mr. Keller is your ex-
husband—although I had no idea when I set up today's
meeting. I never would have asked him to come here if I
had—but if he's willing to invest in The Sugar Shack, as your

financial advisor, I have to recommend that you *seriously* consider his offer. You're doing all right at the moment. The bakery is holding its own. But you'll never be able to move forward with your plans to expand without added capital from an outside source, and if worst comes to worst, one bad season could cause you to lose the business entirely."

Even though Vanessa didn't want to listen, didn't want to believe Brian was right, she knew deep down that he was. The Sugar Shack might be her livelihood, but smart financial planning was his. She wouldn't have begun working with him in the first place if she didn't think he knew what he was doing.

Casting a glance over her shoulder to be sure Marc couldn't overhear their conversation, she turned back and whispered, "There's more at stake here than just the bakery, Brian." So much more. "I'll let him look around. Let the two of you talk. But no matter what kind of plan you two come up with, no matter what offer he might make, I can't promise I'll be willing to accept. I'm sorry."

He looked none too pleased with her assertion, but he nodded, accepting that she would only be pushed so far where Marcus Keller was concerned.

Returning to Marc, Brian informed him of her decision and they started forward again, toward the main entrance of the bakery. The heavenly scents of freshly baked bread, pies and other pastries filled the air the closer they got. As always, those smells caused Vanessa's stomach to rumble and her mouth to water, making her hungry for a piping-hot cinnamon roll or a plate of chocolate chip cookies. Which probably explained why she hadn't quite managed to shed all of her baby weight yet.

At the front door, she stopped abruptly, turning to face the two men. "Wait here," she told them. "I have to warn Aunt Helen that you're in town and explain what's going on. She never particularly liked you," she added, aiming her comment directly at Marc, "so don't be surprised if she refuses to come out while you're here."

He shot her a sardonic grin. "I'll be sure to keep my horns and tail hidden if I run into her."

Vanessa didn't bother responding to that. She was too afraid of what kind of retort might spill from her mouth. Instead, she spun and pushed her way into the bakery.

Keeping a smile on her face and cheerily greeting customers who were sipping cups of coffee, tea or cocoa, and enjoying some of her and her aunt's most popular baked goods, she hurried to the kitchen.

As usual, Helen was bustling around doing this and that. She might have been in her seventies, but she had the energy of a twenty-year-old. Up at the crack of dawn each morning, she always went to work immediately, gathering ingredients, mixing, rolling, cutting, scooping…and managing to keep track of whatever was in the ovens, even three or four different items all set at different temperatures for various amounts of time.

Vanessa was a fairly accomplished baker herself, but readily admitted it took some doing to keep up with her aunt. Add to that the fact that Helen helped her man the counter *and* take care of Danny, and Vanessa literally did not know what she would do without her.

The squeak of the swinging double doors cutting off the kitchen area from the front of the store alerted Helen to her arrival.

"You're back," her aunt said without bothering to look up from the sugar cookies she was dusting with brightly colored sprinkles.

"Yes, but we have a problem," Vanessa told her.

At that, Helen raised her head. "You didn't get the money?" she asked, disappointment lacing her tone.

Vanessa shook her head. "Worse. The investor Brian has me meeting with is Marc."

The container of sprinkles fell from Helen's hand, hitting the metal cookie sheet and spilling everywhere. Not a disaster, just a few cookies that would turn out sloppier than usual. And whatever didn't look appropriate for sale could always go on a plate as an after-dinner treat for themselves.

"You're kidding," her aunt breathed in a shocked voice.

Vanessa shook her head and crossed to where Helen stood rooted to the spot like a statue. "Unfortunately, I'm not. He's outside right now, waiting for a tour of the bakery, so I need you to take Danny upstairs and stay there until I give you the all clear."

Her fingers moved at the speed of light as she undid the knot at Helen's waist, slipping the flour-dusted apron over her head and tossing it aside. Her aunt immediately reached up to pat her stack of puffy, blue-washed curls.

Rushing across the room, Vanessa paused to stare down at her adorable baby boy, who was lying on his back in a small bassinet, doing his best to get his pudgy little toes into his perfect pink mouth. As soon as he saw her, he smiled wide and began to gurgle happily, sending a stab of love so deep through Vanessa's soul, it stole her breath.

Lifting him up and onto her shoulder, she wished she had the time to tickle and tease and coo with him. She loved running the bakery, and was very proud of what she and Aunt Helen had managed to build together, but Danny was her pride and joy. Her favorite moments of the day were those she got to spend alone with him, feeding him, bathing him, making him laugh.

Pressing a kiss to the side of his head, she whispered, "Later, sweetheart, I promise." Just as soon as she could get rid of Marc and Brian.

Turning to her aunt, who had come up behind them, she handed the baby off.

"Hurry," she said. "And keep him as quiet as you can. If he starts to cry, turn on the TV or the radio or something to try to cover it up. I'll get rid of them as quickly as I can."

"All right," Helen readily agreed, "but keep an eye on the ovens. The pinwheel cookies only need another five minutes. The baklava and lemon streusel cake will be a while longer. I set the timers."

Vanessa nodded her understanding, then with Helen bustling off to hide Danny in the small apartment they kept over the bakery, she pushed the now-empty bassinet across the kitchen and into a back storage room. Grabbing an extra white tablecloth with blue and yellow eyelet lace trim, she used it to cover the large piece of telling furniture.

Leaving the storage room, her gaze darted left to right and up and down, searching for any remaining signs of Danny's presence. A few stray items, she might be able to explain...

A rattle? *Oh, a customer must have left it—I'll have to put it in the Lost and Found.*

A handful of diapers? *I keep those on hand for when I watch a friend's baby.* Yes, that sounded plausible.

A half-full bottle in the fridge or a prescription of ear drops in Danny Keller's name from a recent infection? Those might be a little tougher to justify.

She used a clean towel to brush away some of the worst of the spilled sprinkles and grabbed the pinwheels from the oven to keep them from burning, but otherwise left the kitchen as it had been when she'd walked in. Then she pushed back through the double swinging doors into the front of the bakery...and ran smack into a waiting Marcus.

Two

Marc's arms came up to seize Vanessa as she flew through the double doors from the kitchen and hit him square in the chest. The impact wasn't hard enough to hurt, although it did catch him slightly off guard. Then, once he had his hands on her, her body pressed full-length along his own and he didn't want to let go.

It had been a long time since he'd held this woman. Too long, if the blood pounding in his veins and the heat suffusing his groin were any indication.

She was softer than he remembered, more well-rounded in all the right places. But she still smelled of strawberries and cream from her favorite brand of shampoo. And even though she'd cut her hair to shoulder-length, she still had the same wavy copper locks that he knew from experience would be soft as silk against his fingertips.

He nearly reached up to find out for sure, his gaze locked

on her sapphire blue eyes, when she pulled away. He let her go, but immediately missed her warmth.

"I told you to wait outside," she pointed out, licking her glossed lips and running a hand down the front of her snug white blouse. The material pulled taut across her chest, framing her full breasts nicely.

He probably shouldn't be noticing that sort of thing about his ex-wife. But then, he was divorced, not dead.

In response to her chastisement, he shrugged a shoulder. Her annoyance amused him all to hell.

"You were taking too long. And besides, this is a public establishment. The sign in the window says Open. If it upsets you that much, consider me a customer." Reaching into his pocket, he retrieved his money clip and peeled off a couple of small bills. "Give me a cup of black coffee and something sweet. You choose."

Her eyes narrowed and she skewered him with a look of pure disdain. "I told you I don't want your money. Not even that," she added, her gaze flickering to the paltry amount he was holding out to her.

"Have it your way," he told her, sliding the bills back under the gold clip and the entire bundle back into his front trouser pocket. "So why don't you start the tour. Give me an idea of what you do here, how you got started and what your financials look like."

Vanessa blew out a breath, fluttering the thin fringe of her bangs and seeming to come to terms with the fact that she wasn't getting rid of him anytime soon.

"Where's Brian?" she asked, glancing past his shoulder and searching the front of the bakery for her financial advisor.

"I sent him back to his office," Marc answered. "Since he's already familiar with your business, I didn't think it was necessary for him to be here for the tour. I told him I would stop in or call after we've finished."

Tiny lines appeared above Vanessa's nose as she frowned, bringing her attention back to him, though he noticed she wouldn't quite meet his gaze.

"What's the matter?" he teased. "Afraid to be alone with me, Nessa?"

Her frown morphed into a full-fledged scowl, drawing her brows even more tightly together.

"Of course not," she snapped, crossing her arms over her chest, which only managed to lift her generous breasts and press them more snugly against the fabric of her blouse. "But don't get your hopes up, because we *aren't* going to be alone. Ever."

As hard as he tried, Marc couldn't stop an amused grin from lifting his lips. He'd forgotten just what a fiery temper his little wife had, but damned if he hadn't missed it.

If he had anything to say about it, they very well *would* be alone together at some point in the very near future, but he didn't bother saying as much since he didn't want to send her into a full-blown implosion in front of her customers.

"So where do you want to start?" she asked, apparently resigned to his presence and his insistence on getting a look at her bakery as a possible investment opportunity.

"Wherever you like," he acquiesced with a small nod.

It didn't take long for her to show him around the front of the bakery, given its size. But she explained how many customers they could serve in-shop and how much take-out business they did on a daily basis. And when he asked about the items in the display cases, she described every one.

Despite her discomfort at being around him again, he'd never seen her so passionate. While they'd been married, she'd been passionate with him, certainly. The sparks they'd created together had made Fourth of July fireworks look like the flare of a wooden matchstick in comparison.

But outside of the bedroom, she'd been much more

subdued, spending her time at the country club with his mother or working on various charitable committees—also with his mother.

When they met, Vanessa had been in college, not yet decided on a major and he freely admitted that he'd been the driving force behind her *not* graduating with the rest of her class. He'd wanted her too much, been too eager to slip his ring on her finger and make her his—body and soul.

But he'd always expected her to go back to school, and would have supported her a thousand percent, whatever she wanted to do with her life. Somehow, though, she'd gotten distracted and fallen into simply being his wife. A Keller woman whose main purpose was to look good on his arm, add reverence and prestige to the family name, and help raise money for worthy causes.

He wondered now, though, if that's what *she'd* wanted. Or if she'd maybe wanted more than to be simply Mrs. Marcus Keller.

Because while he knew she was proud of the fundraising work she'd done while they were married, she'd never talked about it with this level of enthusiasm in her voice or this much animation to her beautiful features.

He also wondered how well he'd really known his own wife, considering that—with the exception of a few romantic, candlelit meals she'd prepared for him while they were dating—he hadn't even realized she liked to cook or was a world-class baker. But after sampling some of her creations, he decided that if a successful business could stand on its product alone, she may just be sitting on a gold mine.

Finishing the last bite of the banana nut muffin she'd offered, he actually licked his fingers clean, wanting to savor every crumb.

"Delicious," he told her. "So why didn't you ever bake like this while we were married?"

He didn't know if it was his tone—which he'd thought was pleasant enough; he certainly hadn't meant for it to sound accusatory—or the question itself that got her dander up, but she immediately stiffened and took a step away from him, the brief pleasure he'd noted on her face fading away.

"I don't think your mother would have appreciated me messing up her pristine kitchen or getting in Cook's way," she replied tersely. "It might have been the Keller *family* estate, but she runs the place like a monarchy."

No doubt she was right. Eleanor Keller was rather stuck in her ways. Raised in the lap of luxury and used to servants bustling around her, ready to do her bidding, she wouldn't have looked kindly upon her own daughter-in-law doing something as lowly or mundane as preparing a meal or baking desserts, regardless of how talented she might be in that respect.

"You should have done it, anyway," Marc told her.

For a minute, Vanessa didn't reply, though her mouth tightened into a flat line. Then she murmured, "Maybe I should have," before spinning on her heel and leading him away from the counter and display cases.

She pushed through a set of swinging doors painted yellow with The Sugar Shack emblazoned on them in a playful white font and led him into the kitchen. Along with a wave of heat wafting from the industrial ovens lining one wall, the smell of baking was even stronger here, making him hope Vanessa might offer to let him sample a few more items as part of his tour.

While explaining the setup of the kitchen and how she and her aunt shared both baking and front counter duties, she moved around checking timers. Slipping a thick oven mitt on one hand, she began removing cookie sheets and pie pans, setting them on a wide metal island at the center of the room.

"A lot of the recipes are from Aunt Helen's personal

collection," she confided, using a nearby spatula to transfer cookies from sheet to cooling rack. "She's always loved to bake, but had never considered opening her own shop. I couldn't believe she wasn't earning a living with her talents, since everything she makes tastes like heaven. I'm pretty good in the kitchen myself—I must get it from her—" she added with a lopsided grin "—and I guess after a bit, the two of us decided to make a go of it together."

Marc rested his hands on the edge of the island, watching her work. Her movements were smooth and graceful, but also quick and efficient, as though she'd done this a million times before and could do it with her eyes closed, if necessary.

He definitely didn't want to close his eyes, though. He was enjoying the view, struck once again by how much he'd missed being near Vanessa.

The divorce had been so cut and dry, finished almost before he knew what was happening. One minute he'd been married to a beautiful woman he'd adored, thinking everything was fine. The next, she'd announced that she couldn't "live this way anymore" and wanted a divorce. Within a few short months, the papers had been signed and she'd been gone.

Looking back, he admitted that he probably should have fought harder to make their marriage work. At the very least, he should have asked why she was leaving him, what it was she needed that he wasn't giving her.

At the time, however, he'd been busy with the company and the demands of his family and let his pride take the position that he didn't want to be married to any woman who didn't want to be married to him. A part of him, he understood now, had also thought Vanessa was just being dramatic. That she was threatening him with divorce because he hadn't been as attentive to her as she might have wanted, or that once she saw that he wasn't going to put up a fight, she would change her mind and recognize how good she had it.

But that hadn't happened. She hadn't changed her mind and by the time he'd realized she wasn't going to, it had been too late.

"Blake showed me some of your financials," he said, wondering if she'd rap his knuckles with her spatula if he tried to snitch one of the mouthwatering, fresh-from-the-oven cookies. "It looks as though you're doing fairly well."

Without bothering to glance in his direction, she nodded. "We're doing okay. Could be better. We've got a lot of overhead, and the rent for this building wipes us out most months, but we're holding our own."

"Then why are you looking for an investor?"

Finishing up what she was doing, she set aside her spatula and oven mitt, and turned to face him more directly. He noticed, too, that she straightened slightly, shoulders pulling back as though she expected a confrontation.

"I have an idea for expansion," she said slowly, obviously weighing her words carefully. "It's a good idea. I think it will go over well. But it's going to require a bit of construction and more start-up cash than we've got at our disposal."

"So what's the idea?" he wanted to know.

She licked her lips and Marc watched the delicate tendons of her throat convulse as she swallowed before answering. "Mail order. I want to start with a Cookie-of-the-Month Club subscription service that could one day be turned into a catalog business for all of our products."

Judging by the quality of the items he'd tasted so far, he thought it sounded like a damn good prospect. He would certainly consider buying a year's worth of baked goods as quick and easy holiday gifts for numerous family members and business associates. And maybe even one for himself, because he would certainly enjoy a box of The Sugar Shack's cookies showing up on his doorstep once a month.

Not that he told Vanessa as much. Until he decided for sure

whether or not he was going to invest in her and her aunt's little bakery, it was better to keep his thoughts to himself.

"Show me where the construction would take place," he said instead. "I take it you have some back storage area that you could convert, or are maybe thinking of renting the empty building next door?"

She nodded. "The space next door."

Double-checking the rest of the timers and contents of the ovens, she made her way out of the kitchen, trusting Marc to follow. They passed a narrow stairwell outside of the kitchen but tucked away from the front of the shop so that it was nearly invisible to anyone who didn't know it was there.

"Where does that lead?" he asked, inclining his head.

If he wasn't mistaken, he thought Vanessa's eyes went wide and some of the color drained from her face.

"Nowhere," she said quickly. Then, apparently realizing that he would know *something* was at the top of those stairs, she added, "It's just a small apartment. We use it for storage, and as a place for Aunt Helen to nap throughout the day. She wears out easily."

Marc raised a brow. Unless she'd aged exponentially in the year or two since he'd last seen Vanessa's aunt, he found that hard to believe. The woman might be pushing eighty, but there wasn't a bone in her body that could be labeled *old,* and for as long as he'd known her, she'd had the disposition of a hummingbird. But he let it go, deciding that if the building's second story didn't have anything to do with the bakery or his possible investment, then there was nothing up there he needed to know about.

Instead, he allowed her to lead him back through the front of the bakery and outside to the space for rent next door. Though it was locked and they were unable to enter, he could see clearly through the plate glass windows that it was half the size of The Sugar Shack, but completely empty, which meant that there would be very little remodeling necessary to turn it into anything Vanessa wanted. And if his vision of the mail order aspect of the business matched hers, he imagined it wouldn't take much more than a few computers, several packing stations, and a direct and open path connecting it to The Sugar Shack for easy access.

While he continued to peer inside, studying the structure of the connected, unrented area, Vanessa stepped back, standing in the middle of the sidewalk.

"What do you think?" she asked.

He turned to find the afternoon sun glinting off her hair, making it shine like a new penny. A flash of desire hit him square in the chest, nearly knocking him back a pace. His throat clogged and he felt himself growing hard despite the knowledge that he had no right to be attracted to her any longer.

But then, who was he kidding? They might not be married anymore, but he had a feeling it would take a lot more than a signed divorce decree to keep his body from responding to his ex-wife's presence. Something along the lines of slipping into a coma or having a full frontal lobotomy.

Tamping down on the urge to step forward and run his fingers through her mass of copper curls—or do something equally stupid, like kiss her until her knees went weak—he said, "I think you've done very well for yourself." Without him, he was sorry to acknowledge.

She looked only moderately surprised by the compliment. "Thank you."

"I'm going to need some time to look at the books and discuss things with Brian, but if you're not still completely set against working with me, there's a good chance I'd be interested in investing."

If he'd expected squeals of joy or for her to throw herself into his arms in a display of unabashed appreciation, he was doomed to disappointment. She nodded sagely, but otherwise didn't respond.

And he didn't have a reason to stick around any longer.

"Well," he murmured, stabbing his hands into his pockets and rocking back slightly on his heels, "I guess that about does it. Thank you for the tour—and the samples."

Damn, he felt like a teenager out on his first date, and the polite smile she offered only made matters worse.

"I'll be in touch," he told her after a moment of awkward silence.

Tucking a strand of hair behind one ear, Vanessa tipped her head, but said, "I'd prefer you have Brian call me, if you don't mind."

He did mind and a muscle in his jaw ticked as he ground his teeth together to keep from saying so. As much as it annoyed him, though, he understood her reluctance to be in contact with him again. He suspected that even if he offered to sink a boatload of money into Vanessa's enterprise, she might refuse just on principle. A ridiculous principle that would only cause her to end up shooting herself in the foot, but principle all the same.

Vanessa remained on the sidewalk outside The Sugar Shack, watching as Marc walked away, back toward the offices of Blake and Fetzer. Not until he was well out of sight, and she felt sure he wasn't going to turn around and come back, did she let herself release a pent-up breath.

Then, as soon as the pressure in her chest eased and her heart was beating normally again, she spun around and returned to the bakery, heading straight for the stairs that led to the second floor apartment. Halfway up, she heard some of her aunt's favorite 1940s big band music playing, and beneath that, the sound of Danny fussing.

Taking the last several steps two at a time, she hurried in

and found her aunt pacing back and forth across the floor, bouncing and hushing and doing everything she could think of to calm the red-faced child in her arms.

"Poor baby," Vanessa said, reaching for Danny.

"Oh, thank goodness." Helen sighed in relief, more than happy to hand over her squalling charge. "I was just about to give him a bottle, but I know how much you prefer to feed him yourself."

"That's all right, I've got him now," Vanessa told her, continuing to bounce Danny up and down as she moved to the ugly, beige second-hand sofa along the far wall, unbuttoning her blouse as she went. "Thank you so much."

"How did things go? Is Marcus gone now?" Her aunt wanted to know.

"Yes, he's gone."

When the words came out more mumbled than intended, she realized it was because she wasn't entirely pleased with that fact. She might have thought Marc was out of her life for good, and may have been desperate to keep him away once he'd shown up in Summerville unexpectedly, but she realized now that seeing him again hadn't been entirely unpleasant.

One glance from those moss-green eyes and her body went soft and pliant. Her blood turned the consistency of warm honey, her brain functioning about as well as too-flat meringue.

Spending a short amount of time with him while she'd shown him around the bakery had been…not horrible. If it hadn't been for the secret she was hiding just one floor above, she may even have gotten him that cup of coffee and invited him to stay a while longer.

Which was a really bad idea, so it was better that he'd taken off when he had.

She had Danny pressed to her chest, content now that his belly was being filled, when she heard footsteps coming up the stairs. Considering that everyone who knew about the second floor apartment—namely she and Aunt Helen—was already up there, she suspected she was about to get a very rude surprise.

There was no time to jump up and hide the baby, no time to yell for Aunt Helen to run interference. One minute she was glancing around for a blanket to cover her exposed chest, and the next she was frozen in place, staring with alarm at her stunned but furious ex-husband.

Three

Marc honestly didn't know whether to be stunned or furious. Perhaps a mix of both. He wondered if the *whooshing* sound in his ears and the tiny pinpricks of white marring his vision would ever go away.

It wasn't hard to figure out what was going on.

First, Vanessa had lied to him. The space above the bakery wasn't used primarily for storage and as a place for her octogenarian aunt to nap when she started to feel run-down. It was actually a fully furnished and operable apartment, complete with a table and chairs, a sofa, a television…a crib in one corner and a yellow duckie blanket covered with baby toys in the middle of the floor.

Second, Vanessa had a child. She wasn't sitting for a friend; hadn't adopted an infant after their separation just for the thrill of it or to exert her independence. Even if she hadn't been *breast-feeding* the baby in her arms when he'd walked in the room, the protective flare in her eyes and the alarm written all over her face told him everything he needed to know about her connection to the child.

Third and finally, that baby was *his*. He knew it as well as he knew his own name. Felt it, deep down in his bones. Vanessa would never have been so determined to keep him from discovering she was a mother if that weren't the case—if she didn't believe she had something momentous to hide.

Not only that, but he hadn't become the CEO of his family's very successful textile company by being stupid. He could do the math. The only way Vanessa could have such a young infant was if she'd either been pregnant before their divorce had become final or if she'd been cheating on him with another man. And despite the differences that had pushed them apart, infidelity had never been one of them—not by him and not by her.

"Want to tell me what's going on here?" he asked, slipping his hands into the front pockets of his slacks.

It was safer that way. Burying his hands—now curled into tight, angry fists—in his pockets kept him from reaching out to strangle someone. Namely her.

And though his words might have been delivered in the form of a calm, unruffled question, the sharp chill of his tone let her know it was a demand. He wasn't going anywhere until he had answers. All of them.

Out of the corner of his eye, he saw a blur of blue-topped motion as Aunt Helen bustled forward and tossed a blanket over Vanessa's half exposed chest and the baby's head. Marc didn't know which was more disappointing—losing sight of his ex-wife's creamy flesh...or of the child he hadn't known existed until thirty seconds ago.

"I'll be downstairs," Helen murmured to her niece before turning a critical glare on him as she passed. "Yell if you need me."

What Aunt Helen had to be annoyed about, Marc couldn't

fathom. *He* was the victim here. The one who had never been told he was a father, who'd had his child kept from him for so long. He didn't know how old the baby was, exactly, but given the amount of time they'd been divorced and the nine months of her pregnancy, his guess would be about four to six months.

Vanessa and her wily Aunt Helen were the bad guys in this situation. Lying to him. Hiding pertinent facts from him for the past year.

After glancing over his shoulder to be sure they were finally alone, he took another menacing step forward.

"Well?" he prompted.

At first she didn't respond, buying some time by rearranging the lightweight afghan so that it covered her exposed flesh, but not the baby's face. Then with a sigh, she raised her head and met his gaze.

"What do you want me to say?" she asked softly.

Her seeming indifference had his molars grinding together and his fingers curling even tighter, until he thought his knuckles would pop through the skin.

"An explanation might be nice." *Followed by a few hours of abject groveling,* he thought with no small amount of sarcasm, while outwardly he struggled not to let his true level of annoyance show.

"I didn't realize it at the time, but I was pregnant before the divorce became final. We weren't exactly on speaking terms then, so I couldn't find a way to tell you, and to be honest, I didn't think you'd care."

Fury bubbled inside his chest. "Not care about my own child?" he growled. "Not care that I was going to be a father?"

What kind of man did she think he was? And if she could believe he was the sort of man who wouldn't care about his own flesh and blood, why had she bothered to marry him in the first place?

"How do you know it's your baby?" she asked in a low voice.

Marc laughed. A sharp, humorless bark of sound at the sheer ridiculousness of that question.

"Nice try, Vanessa, but I know you too well for that. You wouldn't have broken your vows to have some sleazy, sordid affair. And if you'd met someone you were interested in while we were still married..."

He trailed off, a sudden thought occurring to him that hadn't before. "Is that why you asked for a divorce? Because you met someone else?"

It would be just like her. She would never have cheated on him, never been physically unfaithful. But emotional infidelity was another matter, and toward the end, he had to admit that they hadn't been as close or connected as at the beginning of their relationship.

With his brother as second-in-command, he'd taken over the Keller Corporation and started spending longer and longer hours in the office or traveling for business. Vanessa had complained about feeling lonely and being treated like an outsider in her own home—which was something he could understand, given his mother's less-than-warm nature and the fact that she'd never really cared for the woman he'd married. Hadn't she made that clear from the moment he'd first brought Vanessa home for a visit and announced their engagement?

But even though he'd *heard* Vanessa's complaints, he knew now that he hadn't *listened*. He'd shrugged off her unhappiness, thinking perhaps she was turning into a bit of a bored trophy wife. He'd let himself be consumed by work and told himself it was just a phase—that she'd get over it. He even thought he remembered suggesting she find a hobby to keep her busy in hopes that it would distract her and keep her off his back.

No wonder she'd left him, he mentally scoffed now. *He'd* have left him after being dismissed like that.

By her own husband. The man who was suppose to love, honor and cherish her more than anyone else on the planet. Boy, he'd really messed up on that one, hadn't he?

As always, hindsight was twenty-twenty…and made him want to kick his own ass.

Which meant that if Vanessa *had* met another man, Marc couldn't really blame her for leaving him in hopes of moving into a situation that made her happier than the one she'd been in with him.

The thought of another man touching her, being with her— especially with his baby growing inside her belly—made his vision go red around the edges and his mind fill with images of tearing the aforementioned male who'd dared to touch his woman limb from limb. But he couldn't *blame* her, not when so much of what had gone wrong between them was his own fault.

"Is it?" he asked again, suddenly needing to know. Though he wasn't sure what difference it would make now.

"No," she answered quietly. "There was no one else. Not for me, anyway."

He raised a brow. "What does that mean? That you think *I* was being unfaithful?"

"I don't know, Marc. Were you? It would certainly explain all those extra hours you were supposedly spending at work."

"I had just taken over the company, Vanessa. A lot of things required my attention, practically around the clock."

"And I wasn't one of them, apparently," she muttered, bitterness clear in her tone.

Marc rubbed a spot between his eyes where a headache was

brewing. He'd heard that level of frustration and discontent in her voice before, so many times. The same as he'd heard her complain that he wasn't spending enough time with her.

But what choice did he have? And why couldn't she have cut him some slack? The twenty-four-hour workdays hadn't lasted forever. Nowadays, if he was at the office past five, it was usually because he didn't want to go home. Why bother, when there was nothing much there for him to enjoy other than a soft bed and a giant plasma television?

"This again?" he ground out. "Do we really have to get into this *again?*"

"No," she replied quickly. "That's the nice thing about being divorced—we really don't."

"So that's why you didn't tell me you were pregnant?" he demanded. "Because I wasn't paying enough attention to you before the divorce?"

A furrow appeared in her brow. At her breast, the baby continued to suckle, though he could only hear the sounds, not see the child's mouth actually at work.

"Don't be obtuse," she snapped. "I wouldn't keep something like that from you just because I was pouting or angry with you. If you'll recall, we didn't exactly part on the best terms, and *you* were the one who refused to speak to *me*. That sort of thing makes it difficult to have a personal heart-to-heart."

"You should have tried harder."

Blue eyes flashing, she said, "I could say the same about you."

Marc sighed, rocking back on his heels. It was nice to know that even after a year apart, they could jump right back to where they'd left off.

No growth or progress whatsoever, and to make matters worse, there was a whole new wrench thrown into the works. One with his blood running through its veins. One that he should have been told about from the very beginning.

But arguing with her about it or getting red in the face with fury over having his child kept from him for so long wasn't going to get him anywhere. Not with Vanessa. She would simply argue right back at him and they would end up exactly where they were—in a stalemate.

Striving instead for calm and diplomacy, he said, "I guess that's something we're going to have to agree to disagree about." For now. "But I deserve a few answers, don't you think?"

He could see her mulling that over, trying to decide how much pride or privacy it would cost her to share the details of the last year of her life…and fess up to something he suspected even she knew had been wrong—namely keeping his child from him.

"Fine," she relented after a moment, though she sounded none too pleased with the prospect.

While he weighed his options and tried to decide where to start, she shifted the baby in her arms and quickly rearranged her clothing beneath the veil of the knitted throw to make sure she was completely covered.

The child, Marc noticed, was sound asleep. Eyes closed, tiny pink mouth slack with sleep. And suddenly he knew exactly what he needed to know most of all.

"Is it a boy or a girl?" he asked, his throat clogging with emotion, making the words come out scratchy and thick.

"A boy. His name is Danny."

Danny. Daniel.

His son.

His chest grew tight, cutting off the oxygen to his lungs, and he was glad when Vanessa rose from the sofa, then turned to toss the afghan over the back so she wouldn't see the sudden dampness filling his eyes.

He was a father, he thought, blinking and doing his best

to surreptitiously suck in sharp, quick breaths of air in an attempt to regain his equilibrium.

When he and Vanessa had first gotten married, they'd discussed having children. He'd expected it to happen before long, been ready for it. When it hadn't in the first year, or the second, the idea had drifted further and further to the back of his mind.

And that had been okay. He'd been disappointed, he supposed, but so had she. But they'd still been happy together, still optimistic about the future, and cognizant of the fact that they hadn't even begun to explore all of their options yet. If getting pregnant the fun, old-fashioned way hadn't worked out, he was sure they'd have discussed adoption or in vitro or even fostering.

But as it turned out, they hadn't needed any of that, had they? No, she'd been pregnant when they'd signed the divorce papers.

"When did you find out?" he asked, following her movements as she trailed slowly across the room. The baby— Danny, his son—was propped upright against her shoulder now and she was slowly patting his back, bouncing slightly.

"A month or so after the divorce was final."

"That's why you moved away," he said quietly. "I expected you to stick around Pittsburgh after we split. Then I heard you'd left town, but I never knew where you'd gone." Not that he'd intentionally tried to check up on her, but he'd kept his ear to the ground and—admittedly—welcomed any news he managed to pick up through the grapevine.

She shrugged one slim shoulder. "I had to do something. There was nothing left for me in Pittsburgh and I was soon going to have a child to support."

"You could have come to me," he told her, just barely able to keep the anger and disappointment from seeping into his voice. "I would have taken care of you *and* my child—and you know it."

She stared at him for a moment, but her face was passive, her eyes blank, and he couldn't read her expression.

"I didn't want you to take care of us. Not out of pity or responsibility. We were divorced. We'd already said everything we had to say and gone our separate ways. I wasn't going to put us both back in a position we didn't want to be in just because our reproductive timing was lousy."

"So you came here."

She nodded. "Aunt Helen had only been living here a couple of years herself. She moved in with her sister when Aunt Clara became ill. After she died, Helen claimed the house was too large for one person and she could use the company. Unfortunately, she's never met a problem that couldn't be solved—or at least alleviated—with food, so she baked and I ate. Then one day, I got the brilliant idea that we should open a bakery together. Her recipes are amazing, and I've always been pretty handy in the kitchen myself."

"Good for you," Marc said.

And he meant it. It hurt to realize that he'd never known she had such amazing cooking or baking abilities, or that she'd preferred to move away and live with her aunt in Mayberry R.F.D. over coming to him when she'd discovered her pregnancy.

He certainly had the means to care for her and their son. Even if reconciliation hadn't been an option, he could have set her up in a small house or apartment, somewhere he could visit easily and spend as much time with his child as possible.

He could have provided for her, provided for his child, in ways she could never dream of simply by running a single bakery—no matter how popular—in such a rural area.

But then, Vanessa knew that, didn't she? She was well

aware of his and his family's financial situation. While they'd been married, if she'd asked him to buy her a private island paradise, he could have done so as easily as most people bought a pack of gum.

Which was probably why she'd chosen to move away and find a way to support herself. From the moment they'd met, his money hadn't impressed her. Oh, she'd enjoyed their two week honeymoon in the Greek isles, but she'd never wanted him to give her silly, expensive things just for the sake of it. She'd never wanted priceless jewels or a private jet, or even her own platinum card for unlimited shopping sprees.

When they'd first been married, she hadn't even wanted to move into his family home, despite the fact that his brother and his brother's family resided there and the estate was large enough to house a dozen families comfortably. Possibly without any of them coming into contact with the others for weeks at a time.

Keller Manor boasted a mansion the size of six football fields with separate *wings,* for heaven's sake, as well as three isolated cottages on its surrounding two hundred acres. But Vanessa had wanted to find an apartment of their own in town, then maybe later buy a house for just the two of them and any children that came along.

Marc wondered now if he shouldn't have gone along with her on that idea. At the time, staying at the mansion had been easy, convenient. He'd thought it would be the fastest way for Vanessa to bond with his family and start feeling like a true Keller.

Now, however... Well, considering how well that *hadn't* turned out, he was beginning to think he'd made a lot of wrong decisions while they were together.

After patting the baby on the back for a good five minutes—burping him, Marc assumed—Vanessa moved to a navy blue playpen and started to lean over, presumably to lay Danny down for the rest of his nap.

"Wait," he said, reaching out a hand and taking a step forward before halting in his tracks. What was he doing? Why had he stopped her?

Because he wasn't yet ready to lose sight of his son. Or to be distracted from the reality that he was suddenly a father. A *father.* A fact that part of him still couldn't seem to comprehend.

"Can I hold him?" he asked.

She looked down at the child sleeping in her arms, indecision clear on her face.

"If it won't wake him," he added as an afterthought.

Lifting her head, Vanessa met his gaze. It wasn't fear of waking the baby that caused her hesitation, he realized—it was her fear of having him near their son, of sharing a child who had been hers alone up until now. Not to mention a secret she'd had no intention of sharing anytime soon, but that had been unexpectedly revealed all the same.

Finally, with a sigh, she seemed to reach a decision. Or perhaps come to her senses, since they both knew there was no way he'd be kept from his child now that he was aware of Danny's existence. No way in hell.

"Of course," she said, the words sounding much more agreeable than she felt, he was sure. Meeting him halfway, she carefully transferred the child from her arms to his.

The last child Marc had held who was this size, this age, had to have been his three-year-old niece. But as adorable as his brother's children were, as much as he loved them, it didn't hold a candle to how he felt now, cradling *his own* child to his chest.

He was so tiny, so beautiful, so amazingly peaceful in sleep. Marc soaked in every minuscule feature, from the light dusting of brown hair covering Danny's head to his satin-soft cheeks, to the tiny fingers he curled and uncurled just beneath his chin.

Marc tried to imagine how Danny had looked as soon as he'd been born…his first day home from the hospital…how Vanessa had looked all rounded and glowing in pregnancy. Tried and failed, because he hadn't been there, hadn't known.

A furrow of irritation drew his brows together and he knew he couldn't leave Summerville without his son, without spending more time with him and hearing every detail of the months that he'd missed of this child's life.

Drawing his attention back to Vanessa, he said, "It looks like we've got a bit of a problem here. I've been left out of the loop and have some catching up to do. So I'm going to give you two choices."

Before she could interrupt, he pressed on. "You and Danny can either pack a bag and come back to Pittsburgh with me, or you can give me an excuse to stick around here. But either way, I *will* be staying with my son."

Four

Vanessa wanted nothing more than to snatch Danny away from Marc and go running. Find a place to hide herself and her baby until he lost interest and went back from whence he came.

She knew her ex-husband better than that, though, didn't she? He would be more inclined to give up breathing or walking upright than he would to walk away from his child.

There was nowhere she could go, nowhere she could hide that he wouldn't find her. So she might as well save herself the time and trouble and just face the music. She'd composed the symphony, after all.

She'd also been prepared to tell him about her pregnancy as soon as she'd discovered it for herself. Just because things hadn't worked out quite the way she'd planned didn't mean she should disregard her moral values now.

But that didn't mean she was ready to pack up and follow

him back to Pittsburgh like a lost puppy. She had a life here. Family, friends, a business to run.

On the other hand, the thought of Marc staying in Summerville made her heart palpitate and brought her as close to suffering a panic attack as she'd ever felt. How could she possibly handle having him underfoot—at the bakery and maybe even living with them at Aunt Helen's house?

She was trapped between the proverbial rock and a hard place, both of which looked suspiciously like her ex-husband. Stubborn, stoic, amazingly handsome in a suit and tie.

"I can't go back to Pittsburgh," she blurted out, pretending the sight of Marc holding their infant son in his big, strong arms didn't tug at parts of her that had no business being tugged.

"Fine," he said with a nod, his face resolute and jaw firm. "Then I guess I'm relocating."

Oh, no, that was worse. Wasn't it? Rock, hard place... rock, hard place. Her chest was so tight with panic, she was beginning to see stars from lack of oxygen.

"You can't stay here forever," she told him. "What about the company? Your family?" My sanity?

"It won't be forever," he responded.

Looking more reluctant than she'd ever seen him, he handed Danny back to her, careful not to wake him. Then he reached into his jacket pocket and removed a slim black cell phone.

"But if you think that anything back home—with the company or my family—is more important than being here with my son right now, you're crazy. I can afford to take a few weeks away, I just have to make sure everyone knows where I am and can keep things running smoothly in my absence."

With that, he turned and headed for the stairs leading back down to the bakery, dialing as he went.

Rocking back and forth, Vanessa stared down at her sleeping son and felt tears prickle behind her eyes.

"Oh, baby," she whispered, pressing a kiss to his smooth forehead. "We're in so much trouble."

For Vanessa, having Marc "move" to Summerville felt very much like when she'd first met him.

She'd been putting herself through school by waiting tables at an all-night diner near the college campus. He'd been attending school on his father's dime, breezing through classes and spending his free time playing football or attending frat parties.

He'd walked into the diner late one night with a pack of his friends, all of whom could have been male models for some brand of expensive cologne or another. She'd served them pancakes and eggs, and enough soda to float the *Titanic*. And even though she'd noticed him—she'd noticed all of them; how could she not?—she hadn't thought much of it. Why should she, when he was just one of a thousand different customers she served day in and day out? Not to mention one of the many young, carefree men who breezed through school—and life, it seemed—while she worked her fingers to the bone and burned the candle at both ends just trying to *stay* in school?

But then he'd shown up again. Sat in her section again. Sometimes with friends, other times by himself.

He'd smiled at her. Left huge tips, sometimes a hundred percent in addition to his check total. And made small talk with her. It wasn't until much later that she realized she'd told him nearly her entire life story in bits and pieces over a matter of weeks.

Finally, he'd asked her out and she'd been too enamored to say no. Half in love with him already and well on her way to head over heels.

Those same sensations were swamping her now. Shock, confusion, trepidation… He was a force to be reckoned with, much like a natural disaster. He was a tornado, an earthquake, a tsunami swooping in and turning her entire life upside down.

Within the hour, he'd been in touch with everyone he'd needed to contact back in Pittsburgh. Put out the word that he would be staying in Summerville indefinitely, and that his right-hand men—and women—were in charge of Keller Corp until further notice.

As far as Vanessa knew, though, he hadn't told them why he would be away for a while. She'd overheard him on the phone with his brother, but all Marc had said was that the business he was thinking of investing in looked promising and he needed to stick around to take a closer look at the premises and financials.

Keeping the true reason to himself was probably a smart move, she admitted reluctantly. No doubt if Eleanor Keller learned that her cherished son had a child with his evil ex-wife, she would go into a tizzy of epic proportions. Her already just-sucked-on-a-lemon expression would turn even more pinched and she would immediately begin plotting ways to get both Marc and Danny back into her circle of influence.

But not Vanessa. Eleanor would be plotting ways to *keep* Vanessa from reentering her or her son's lives.

Vanessa imagined that where Marc took it as a given that he was Danny's father, Marc's mother would insist on having a paternity test conducted as soon as possible. She would pray for a result that proved Danny was another man's child, of course, leaving Marc free and clear.

Free and clear of Vanessa, and free and clear to marry someone else. A woman Eleanor would not only approve of, but would probably handpick herself.

She didn't verbalize her inhospitable thoughts to Marc, however. He didn't know how truly horrid his mother had been to her while they'd been married and she saw no reason to enlighten him now.

"There," he said, pushing through the swinging door into the kitchen where she and Aunt Helen were keeping themselves busy. He slipped his cell phone into his pocket, then shrugged out of his suit jacket altogether.

"That should buy me a few weeks of freedom before the place starts to fall apart and they send out a search party."

Aunt Helen was up to her elbows in bread flour, but her feelings on the subject of Marc staying in town were clear in the narrow slits of her eyes and the force she was using to knead the ball of dough in front of her.

She didn't like it one little bit, but as Vanessa had told her while Marc was making phone calls, they didn't have a choice. Either Marc stuck around until he got whatever it was that he was after, or he would drag Vanessa and Danny back to Pittsburgh.

She'd considered a third option—sending Marc back to Pittsburgh on his own—but knew that if she pushed him on the issue, it would only cause trouble and hostility. If she refused to allow Marc time with his son, in one town or another, Vanessa had no doubt it would only spur her ex-husband to throw his weight and his family's millions around.

And what did that mean? A big, ugly custody battle.

She was a good mother, so she knew Marc could never take Danny away from her on that basis alone. But she didn't fool herself, either, that the system wouldn't be swayed by the amount of money and power the Kellers could bring to bear. Eleanor alone wasn't above bribery, blackmail or making up a series of stories to paint Vanessa in the most negative light possible.

No, if there was any way to avoid a custody fight or any amount of animosity with Marc whatsoever, then she had to try. It might even mean making arrangements for shared custody and traveling back and forth to Pittsburgh or having Marc travel back and forth to Summerville. But whatever it took to keep Marc happy and Danny with her, she would do.

Even if it meant letting her ex move into her life—and her business and possibly her house—for God knew how long.

Finished filling a tray with fresh squares of turtle brownies, Vanessa wiped her hands on a nearby dish towel. "What about your things?" she asked. "Don't you need to go home and collect your personal items?"

Marc shrugged, and she couldn't help but notice the shift of firm muscle beneath his white button-down shirt. She remembered only too well what lay beneath that shirt, and how much she'd once enjoyed knowing it belonged to her and her alone.

"I'm having some clothes and such shipped. Anything else I need, I'm sure I can purchase here."

He hung his jacket on a hook near the door, where she and Helen kept their aprons when not in use, then crossed to the bassinet she'd dragged back out of the storeroom once Marc had figured out what was going on. Danny was sleeping inside, stretched out on his little belly, arms and legs all akimbo.

"The only question now," Marc said, gazing down at his son, then reaching out to stroke a single finger over Danny's soft cheek, "is where I'll be staying while I'm in town."

Vanessa opened her mouth, not even sure what she was about to say, only to be interrupted by Helen.

"Well, you're not staying in my house," her aunt announced in no uncertain terms. Her tight, blue-washed curls bobbed as she used the heels of her hands to beat the ball of bread dough into submission.

Though her aunt's clear dislike of Marc brought an immediate stab of guilt and the sudden urge to apologize, Vanessa was unaccountably grateful that Helen had the nerve to blurt out what she'd been unable to find the courage to tell him herself.

"Thank you so much for the kind invitation," Marc said, lips twisted with amusement, "but I really couldn't impose."

How typical of him to take Helen's rudeness in stride. That sort of thing never had fazed him, mainly because Marc knew who he was, where he came from and what he could do.

Plus, Aunt Helen hadn't always hated him. She didn't hate him now, actually, she was just annoyed with him and took his treatment of Vanessa personally.

Which was at least partly Vanessa's fault. She'd shown up on her aunt's doorstep hurt, angry, broken and carrying her ex-husband's child.

After spilling out the story of her rocky marriage, subsequent divorce, unexpected pregnancy and desperate need for a place to stay—with Marc filling the role of bad guy-slash-mean old ogre under the bridge at every turn—her aunt's opinion of him had dropped like a stone. Ever since then, Aunt Helen's only objective was to *not* see her niece hurt again.

Vanessa was still fighting the urge to make excuses for Helen when Marc said, "I thought maybe you could recommend a nice local hotel."

Vanessa and Helen exchanged a look.

"Guess that would be the Harbor Inn just a couple streets over," Helen told him. "It's not much, but your only other option is Daisy's Motel out on Route 12."

"Harbor Inn," Marc murmured, brows drawing together. "I

didn't realize there was a waterway around here large enough to necessitate a harbor."

Vanessa and Helen exchanged another look, along with mutual ironic smiles.

"There isn't," Vanessa told him. "It's one of those small town oddities that no one can really explain. There's no harbor nearby. Not even a creek or stream worth mentioning. But the Harbor Inn is one of Summerville's oldest hotels, and it's decorated top to bottom with lighthouses, seagulls, fishing nets, starfish…"

She shook her head, hoping Marc wouldn't think too badly of the town or its residents. Even though some parts were a little backward at times, this was her home now and she found herself feeling quite protective toward it.

"If nothing else, it's an amusing place to stay," she added by way of explanation.

He looked less than convinced, but didn't say anything. Instead, he moved away from the bassinet and started to unbutton his cuffs, rolling the sleeves of his shirt up to his elbows.

"As long as it has a bed and a bathroom, I'm sure it will be fine. I'll be spending most of my time here with you, anyway."

Vanessa's eyes widened at that. "You will?"

One corner of his mouth quirked. "Of course. This is where my son is. Besides, if your goal is to expand the bakery and possibly branch out into mail-order sales, we've got a lot to discuss, and possibly a lot to do."

"Wait a minute." She let the spatula in her hand drop to the countertop, feeling her breath catch. "I didn't agree to let you have anything to do with The Sugar Shack."

He flashed her a charming, confident grin. "That's why we have so much to discuss. Now," he said, flattening his palms on the edge of the counter, "are you going to show me to this Harbor-less Inn, or would you prefer to simply give me directions so you and your aunt can both stay here and talk about me after I leave?"

Oh, she wanted to stay behind and talk about him. The problem was, he knew it. And now that he'd tossed down the gauntlet by effectively *telling* her he knew that's exactly what would happen the minute he left the room, she had no choice but to go with him.

Which was exactly why he'd done it.

Reaching behind her back, she untied the strings of her apron and pulled it off over her head.

"I'll take you," she said, then turned to her aunt. "Will you be okay on your own while we're gone?"

The question was just a formality; there were plenty of times when Vanessa left Helen in charge of the bakery while she ran errands or took Danny to the pediatrician. Still, her aunt shot her such a contemptible look that Vanessa nearly chuckled.

"All right. I'll be back in a bit."

She headed for the door, saying to Marc as she passed, "I just need to grab my purse."

He followed her out, waiting at the bottom of the stairs while she ran up to collect her purse and sunglasses.

"What about the baby?" he asked as soon as she returned.

"He'll be fine."

"Are you sure your aunt can take care of him *and* the bakery at the same time?" He pressed as they moved past the store-front's display cases and small round tables toward the door.

Vanessa smiled and waved at familiar customers as she passed. Once outside, she slipped on her sunglasses before turning to face him.

"Don't let Helen hear you asking something like that. She's liable to hurl a cookie sheet at your head."

He didn't laugh. In fact, he didn't look amused at all. Instead, he looked legitimately concerned.

"Relax, Marc. Aunt Helen is extremely competent. She runs the bakery by herself all the time."

"But—"

"*And* watches Danny at the same time. We both do. Truthfully, she's been a godsend," Vanessa admitted. "I don't know what I'd do without her."

Or what she would have *done* without her, when she'd found herself jobless, husbandless and pregnant all in the space of a few short months.

"So are we taking your car or mine?" she asked in an attempt to draw Marc's focus away from worrying about Danny.

"Mine," he said.

Vanessa kept pace with him as he turned on his heel and started down the sidewalk in the direction of Blake and Fetzer where he'd left his Mercedes. She was still dressed in the skirt and blouse she'd worn for her disastrous meeting earlier that morning. She wished now that she'd taken the time to change into something more comfortable. She especially wished she'd exchanged her heels for a pair of flats.

Marc, however, looked as suave and at ease as ever in his tailored suit pants and polished dress shoes. His jacket was slung over one shoulder, his other hand tucked casually into his slacks.

When they reached his car, he held the door while she climbed in the front passenger side, then rounded the back and slid in behind the wheel. He slipped the key in the ignition, then sat back in his seat, turning to face her.

"Will you do something for me before we head for the hotel?" he asked.

A shiver of trepidation skated beneath her skin and she immediately tensed. Hadn't she already done enough?

Wasn't she already *doing* enough simply by accepting Marc's presence in town when what she really wanted to do was snatch up her child and head for the hills?

She also couldn't help remembering the many times they'd been alone in a car together in the past. Their first dates, where they'd steamed up the windows with their passion. After they were married, when a simple trip to the grocery store or out to dinner would include soft, intentional touches and comfortable intimacy.

She was sure he remembered, too, which only added to the tightening of her stomach and nervous clench of her hands on the strap of her purse where it rested on her lap.

"What?" she managed to say, holding her breath for the answer.

"Show me around town. Give me the ten-dollar tour. I don't know how long I'll be here, but you can't be dropping everything every time I need directions."

Vanessa blinked and released her breath. Okay, that wasn't nearly as traumatizing as she'd expected. It was actually rather thoughtful of him.

Since her mouth had gone dry, for a second she could only lick her lips and bob her head in agreement. With an approving nod, he started the car and began to pull out of the lot.

"Which way?" he asked.

It took her a moment to think of where to start, and what she should show him, but Summerville was so small that she finally decided it wouldn't hurt to show him pretty much everything.

"Take a left," she told him. "We'll do Main Street, then I'll take you around the outskirts. We should end up at the Harbor Inn without too much backtracking."

A lot of the local businesses he could make out for himself. The diner, the drugstore, the flower shop, the post office. A little farther from the center of town were a couple of fast-food restaurants, gas stations and a Laundromat. In between the smattering of buildings were handfuls of houses, farms and wooded parcels.

She told him a bit of what she knew about her neighbors, both the owners of neighboring businesses and some of the residents of Summerville.

Like Polly—who ran Polly's Posies—and went around town every morning to deliver a single fresh flower to each store on Main Street free of charge. The vase she'd provided Vanessa was front and center on the counter, right next to the cash register, and even though she never knew what kind of flower Polly would choose to hand out on any given day, she had to admit the tiny dot of color really did add a touch of hominess to every single business in town.

Or Sharon—the pharmacist at Main Street Drugs—who had given Vanessa such wonderful prenatal advice and even set her up with her current pediatrician.

She had such close relationships with so many people in town. Something she'd never had while living in Pittsburgh with Marc. In the city, whether visiting the grocery store, pharmacy or dry cleaner's, she'd been lucky to make eye contact with the person behind the counter, much less make small talk.

Here, there was no such thing as a quick trip to the store. Every errand involved stopping numerous times to say hello and catch up with friendly acquaintances. And while she'd never missed that sort of thing before, she knew she would definitely miss it now if she woke up one day and realized it was no longer a part of her life.

"That's about it," she told him twenty minutes later, after pointing him in the general direction of the hotel where he would be staying. "There isn't much more to see, unless you're interested in a tour of the dairy industry from the inside out."

A small smile curved his lips. "I'll pass, thanks. But I think you missed something."

She frowned, wondering what he could possibly mean. She hadn't shown him the nearest volunteer fire department or water treatment plant, but those were several miles outside of town, and she didn't think he really cared about that sort of thing, anyway.

"You didn't show me where *you* live," he supplied in a low voice.

"Do you really need to know?" she asked, ignoring the spike of heat that suffused her from head to toe at the knowing glance he sent her.

"Of course. How else will I know where to pick you up for dinner?"

Five

As much as Vanessa would have liked to argue with Marc about his heavy-handedness, in the end, she didn't bother. He had a nasty habit of getting his way in almost every situation, anyway, so what was the point?

She'd also reluctantly decided that, for as long as Marc was determined to stay in her and Danny's lives, it was probably better to simply make nice with him. There was no sense antagonizing him or fighting him at every turn when he potentially held so much of her future in his hands.

At the moment, the only thing he seemed to want was time with and information about his son. He wasn't trying to take Danny away from her or making threats about trying to take him later, even though they both knew he was probably within his rights to do so.

The threatening part, not the actual taking. But if she were in his shoes, anger and a sense of betrayal alone would have had her yelling all manner of hostile, menacing things.

So this afternoon when Marc asked her to show him where she lived with Aunt Helen, she took him to the small, two-story house on Evergreen Lane. It wasn't much compared to the sprawling estate where he'd grown up with servants and tennis courts and a half mile, tree-lined drive just to reach the front gate, but in the last year, it had become home to her.

Helen had given up her guest room to Vanessa and helped turn her sewing room into a nursery for Danny. She'd volunteered her kitchen to thousands of hours of trial and error with her family recipes before they'd felt brave enough to move forward with the idea of actually opening a bakery of their very own.

In return, Vanessa helped with the general upkeep of the house, had planted rows of brand-new pink and red begonias in the flower beds lining the front porch and walk, and had even taught Helen enough about computers to have her emailing with friends from grade school she'd never thought to be in contact with again.

Though Vanessa still believed there was no way she could ever truly repay her aunt's kindness in her time of need, Helen insisted she enjoyed the company and was happy to have so much youth and activity in the house again. Which, in Vanessa's book, made the tiny white house on less than an acre of mottled green and yellow grass more of a home than Keller Manor, with all its bells and whistles, could ever be.

Taking a deep breath, she checked herself over in the bathroom mirror one last time—though she wasn't sure why she bothered. Yes, it had been a while since she'd had a reason to get so dressed up, let alone get so dressed up twice in one day.

But even though jeans and tennies were more her style these days, Marc had seen her in everything from ratty shorts and T-shirts to full-length ball gowns and priceless jewels.

Besides, she wasn't attempting to impress him this evening, was she? No, she was pacifying him.

After showing him to the Harbor Inn and then letting him drop her off at The Sugar Shack once again, Vanessa had finished off her day at the bakery, closed up shop, and headed home with Danny and her aunt. While Helen had fixed dinner for herself and kept Danny entertained, Vanessa had run upstairs to change clothes and retouch her makeup.

She wasn't fixing herself up for Marc, she told her reflection. She wasn't. It was simply that she was taking advantage of a dinner invitation that included the chance to look like a woman for a change instead of a frazzled working mother struggling to be a successful entrepreneur.

That's the only reason she was wearing her favorite strapless red dress, strappy red heels and dangling imitation ruby earrings. It was over-the-top for even the priciest restaurant in Summerville, but she didn't care. She might never get the opportunity to wear this outfit again...or to remind Marc of just what he'd given up when he let her go.

The doorbell rang before she was ready for it and her heart lurched in her chest. She quickly swiped on another layer of lipstick, then made sure she had everything she needed in the tiny red clutch she'd dug out of the back of her closet.

Halfway down the stairs, she heard voices and knew Aunt Helen had answered the door in her absence. She didn't know whether to be grateful or nervous about that; it depended, she supposed, on Aunt Helen's current disposition.

At the bottom of the landing, she found Aunt Helen standing inside the open door, one hand on the knob. No shotgun or frying pan in sight, which was a good sign.

Marc stood on the other side of the door, still on the porch. He was dressed in the same charcoal suit as earlier, forest-green tie arrow straight and jacket buttoned back in place. His hands were linked behind his back and he was smiling down at Aunt Helen with all the charm of a used car salesman. When he spotted her, Marc transferred that dimpled grin to her.

"Hi," he said. "You look great."

Vanessa resisted the urge to smooth a hand down the front of her dress or recheck the knot of her upswept hair. "Thank you."

"I was just telling your aunt what a lovely home she has. At least from the outside," he added with a wink, likely because Aunt Helen had obviously failed to invite him inside.

"Would you like to come in?" Vanessa asked, ignoring her aunt's sidelong scowl.

"Yes, thank you." Marc ignored the scowl, too, brushing past Aunt Helen and into the entranceway.

He gave the house a cursory once-over and Vanessa wondered if he was comparing it to his own lavish residence, possibly finding it lacking as an appropriate place for his child to be raised. But when he turned back, his expression held no censure, only mild curiosity.

"Where's Danny?" he asked.

"The kitchen," Helen supplied, closing the front door, then moving past them in that direction. "I was just giving him his dinner."

Marc shot Vanessa a glance before waving her ahead of him as they followed Helen through the living area to the back of the house. "I thought you were still breast-feeding."

She flushed, feeling heat climb over her cheeks toward her hairline. "I am, but not exclusively. He also gets juice, cereal and a selection of baby food."

"Good," he murmured with a short nod, watching as Aunt Helen rounded the kitchen table and took a seat. "The longer a child breast-feeds, the better. It increases immunity, builds the child's sense of security and helps with mother/child bonding."

"And how do you know that?" she asked, genuinely surprised.

Danny was strapped into his Winnie the Pooh swing, face and bib spattered with a mixture of strained peas, strained carrots and applesauce. He looked like a Jackson Pollock painting as he kicked his feet and slapped his hands against the plastic sides of the seat that held him.

Without waiting for an invitation, Marc sat down opposite Aunt Helen, leaning in to rub Danny's head. The baby giggled and Marc grinned in return.

"Contrary to popular belief," he murmured, not bothering to turn in her direction, "I didn't become CEO of Keller Corp by nepotism alone. I actually happen to be quite resourceful when I need to be."

"Let me guess—you dug out your laptop and hit the internet."

"I'm not telling," he answered, tossing her a teasing half smile. Then to Aunt Helen, he said, "May I?" indicating the array of baby food jars spread out in front of her.

The older woman gave him a look that clearly said she didn't think he was capable, but she waved him on all the same. "Be my guest."

He picked up the miniature plastic spoon with a cartoon character on the handle and began feeding Danny in tiny bites, waiting long enough in between them for the baby to gum and smack and swallow.

Vanessa stood back, watching…and wishing. Wishing she hadn't agreed to go out to dinner with Marc this evening, after all. Wishing she hadn't invited him in and that he hadn't wanted to see Danny before they left. Wishing this whole scene wasn't so domestic, so bittersweet, so much of a reminder of what could have been.

Marc looked entirely too comfortable feeding his son, even dressed as he was in a full business suit. He was also oddly good at it, which she wouldn't have expected from a man who hadn't spent much time around babies before.

When Danny began to fuss and wouldn't take another bite, Marc set aside the jars and spoon, and brushed his hands together.

"I'd like to pick him up for a minute," he said, splitting his gaze between his expensive suit and his infant son, who was doing his best imitation of a compost pile, "but…"

"Definitely not," Vanessa agreed, grabbing a damp cloth to wipe the worst of the excess food from Danny's mouth and chin. "Let Aunt Helen get him cleaned up and maybe you can hold him when we get back, if he's still awake."

Marc didn't look completely pleased with that idea, but since the alternative was ruining a suit that probably cost more than most people's monthly mortgage payment, he wisely refrained from reaching out and getting covered by Gerber's finest.

"Shouldn't we go?" she prompted as he pushed to his feet and Aunt Helen rounded the table to scoop Danny from the swing.

Still looking reluctant to leave, Marc nodded and followed her back through the house to the front door. Outside, he led her to his car, which was parked at the curb, and helped her inside.

"What do you do when he's a mess like that?" Marc asked once he'd climbed in beside her.

She twisted in her seat to face him, noticing the frown pulling at the corners of his mouth. "What do you mean?"

"How do you not pick up your own child?"

Vanessa blinked, wondering if she'd heard him correctly. Oh, she heard the words clearly enough, but was that a hint of guilt stealing through his tone? *Guilt* from a man she hadn't thought understood the concept? Who'd let her walk away without a fight, with barely an explanation?

"Marc." Shaking her head, she ducked her chin to keep him from seeing the amusement tugging at her lips. "I know this is all new to you. I know finding out about Danny was quite a shock, but you have nothing to feel guilty about. He's a baby. As long as all of his needs are met, he doesn't care who's feeding him, who's holding him, who's changing his diaper."

If anything, Marc's frown deepened. "That isn't true. Infants know the difference between their parents and simply a babysitter, between their mother and their father."

"All right," she acquiesced, "but rest assured that there are plenty of times I don't pick him up right after he's eaten because I don't want him to get food on my clothes. Or worse yet, yurk on me."

"Yurk?"

"It's what Aunt Helen and I call a 'yucky burp,'" she explained, wrinkling her nose in distaste. "Believe me, once you've had soured milk or formula spit up all over you, you learn fast not to wear nice clothes around a baby and to keep a towel handy."

Without a thought of what she was doing, she reached across the console and patted his thigh. "If you're going to be in town for a while to spend time with him, get yourself some nice, cheap jeans and T-shirts, and expect them to get dirty on a regular basis. But don't worry about tonight. I didn't hold him this morning, either, because I was dressed up for my meeting with you. That's one of the great things about having Aunt Helen around. I can't do everything all by myself and she helps to pick up the slack."

Meeting her gaze, Marc wrapped his fingers around hers, holding her hand in place, even when she tried to pull it away. "I should be the one helping you with Danny, not your aunt. But don't worry, we're going to talk about that over dinner. Among other things."

* * *

Despite the threat of The Big Talk and being pinned to her chair like a bug under Marc's intense scrutiny and personal version of the Spanish Inquisition, dinner was actually quite enjoyable. He took her to the hotel's dining room, which was actually one of the more moderately upscale restaurants in town and attempted to ply her with wine and crab cakes. Of course, since she was breast-feeding, the wine was a no-no, but the crab cakes were delicious. Maybe because he let her eat them in peace.

As soon as the waitress topped off their coffees and they'd made their dessert selections, however, she knew the stay of execution was over. Marc cupped his hands around the ceramic mug and leaned forward in his seat, causing her to tense slightly in her own.

"What was the pregnancy like?" he asked, getting straight to the point, as usual.

Vanessa blew out a small breath, relieved that he was at least starting out with an easy question instead of immediately launching into demands and ugly accusations.

"It was pretty typical, I think," she told him. "Bearing in mind I'd never been pregnant before and didn't really know what to expect. But there were no complications and even the morning sickness wasn't too bad. It didn't always limit itself to mornings, which made getting the bakery open and working twelve-hour days a bit of an adventure," she added with a chuckle, "but it wasn't as terrible as I'd expected."

From there he wanted to know every detail of Danny's birth. Date, time, length, weight, how long her labor had lasted—all facts that she'd taken for granted. In his shoes, though, she could imagine how desperate she would be to learn and memorize every one of them.

"I should have been there," he said softly, staring down at

the table. Then he lifted his gaze to hers. "I *deserved* to be there. For all of it."

Her heart lurched and she braced herself for the onslaught, for every bit of anger and resentment she knew he had to be feeling…and that she probably deserved. But instead of lashing out, his voice remained level.

"As much as it bothers me, there's no going back, we can only move forward. So here's the deal, Vanessa."

His green eyes bore into her, the same look she suspected he gave rival business associates during mergers and tricky acquisitions.

"Now that I know about Danny, I want in on everything. I'll stick around here for a while, until you get used to that idea. Until I get the hang of being a father and he starts to recognize me that way. But after that, I'm going to want to take him home."

At that, at the mention of his home, not hers, Vanessa went still, her shoulders stiffening and her fingers tightening on the handle of her coffee cup.

"That's not a threat," he added quickly, obviously noticing how tense her body had gone. "I'm not saying I want to take him back to Pittsburgh forever. I honestly don't know yet how we're going to work out the logistics of that, but we can discuss it later. I'm only talking about a visit so I can introduce him to my family, let my mother know she has another grandchild."

Oh, Eleanor would love that, Vanessa thought with derision. She'd be thrilled with another grandchild, especially another *male* grandchild to carry on the Keller name. But that grandchild's mother was another story—and Marc's mother would only truly be happy with Vanessa out of the picture.

"And what if I don't agree? To any of it?"

One dark brow winged upward. "*Then* I'll be forced to threaten, I suppose. But is that really the direction you want to go? I've been pretty amicable about this entire situation so far, even though I think we both know I have more than enough reason to be furious over it."

Taking a sip of his coffee, he tipped his head to the side, looking much calmer than she felt.

"If you want me to be furious and toss around ugly threats you know I can follow through on, that's fine, just say the word. But if you'd rather act like two mature adults determined to create the best environment possible for their child, then I suggest you go along with my plans."

"Do I have a choice?" she grumbled, understanding better than ever the adage about being stuck between a rock and a hard place.

Marc's smile was equal parts cocky and confident. "You had the choice of whether or not to tell me you were pregnant in the first place, and you decided not to, so…not really. The ball is in my court now."

Six

The ball was most definitely in Marc's court—along with everything else. But then, she'd known that the minute he'd walked up the stairs to the bakery's second-floor apartment and discovered he had a son, hadn't she? Her only option now was to play nice and hope he would continue to do the same.

Marc's hand was on her elbow as they left the restaurant, guiding her along the carpeted passage toward the lobby. Old fishing nets and decorative life preservers lined the walls and she suddenly realized how odd the decor must seem to outsiders.

Those who were familiar with Summerville never gave it a second thought, but anyone coming into town for the first time must wonder at the hotel's name and decor without a significant body of water nearby to back them up. Especially since the hotel's dining room didn't even particularly specialize in seafood dishes.

"Come upstairs with me," he murmured suddenly just above her ear.

Tearing her gaze from a large plastic swordfish caught in one of the nets, she flashed Marc a startled, disbelieving look, only to have him chuckle at her reaction.

"That isn't a proposition," he assured her, then waggled his eyebrows in an exaggerated attempt at flirtation. "Although I wouldn't be opposed to a bit of after-dinner seduction."

At the lobby, he steered her to the left, away from the hotel's main entrance and in the direction of the wide, *Gone with the Wind*-esque stairwell that led to the guest rooms.

"I have something to show you," he continued as they slowly climbed the stairs, her heels digging into the thick carpeting, faded in places from years of wear.

"Now that sounds like a proposition. Or maybe a bad pickup line," she told him.

He slanted her a grin, digging into his pocket for the key to his room. Not a key card, but an honest to goodness key, complete with a giant plastic fob in the shape of a lighthouse.

"You know me better than that. I didn't need cheesy pickup lines with you the first time around, I don't need them now."

No, he hadn't. He'd been much too charming and suave to hit on her the way ninety percent of guys did back then. Which was only one of the things that had made him more appealing, made him stand out from the pack.

When they reached his door, he unlocked it, then stepped back to let her pass into the room ahead of him. She'd visited the Harbor Inn before, of course, but had never actually been in one of the guest rooms, so for a second she stood just inside the door, taking in her surroundings.

Even if the large brass plaque on the front of the building hadn't identified the hotel as a historical landmark, she would have known it was old simply from the interior. The elaborately carved woodworking, the barely preserved wallpaper and the antique fixtures all would have tipped her off. Certain things had been updated, of course, to keep the hotel functional and modern enough that guests would be comfortable, but a lot had been left or restored to maintain as much of the original furnishings and adornments as possible.

Marc's room was blissfully lacking in the oceanside motif. Instead, the walls boasted tiny pink roses on yellowing wallpaper, and both the single window and four-poster bed were covered in white eyelet lace. Very old-fashioned and grandmotherly.

It was almost funny to see tall, dark, modern businessman Marc standing in the middle of all the extremely formal, nineteenth century finery. He looked completely out of place, like a zebra in the dolphin enclosure at the zoo.

But *looking* out of place and *being* out of place were two different things, and Marc didn't seem to feel the least bit out of place. Closing the door behind them, he shrugged out of his charcoal suit jacket and tossed it over the back of a burgundy brocade wing chair on his way to the brass-plated desk against the far wall.

While he lifted the lid of his laptop and hit the button to boot up the computer, Vanessa stood back and enjoyed the view. Shallow of her, she was sure. Not to mention inconsistent, considering how vehemently she protested—to herself and anyone else who would listen—that the divorce had been a blessing and she was over him. Completely and totally over him.

Being his *ex*-wife didn't keep her from being a living, breathing, red-blooded woman, however. And every one of the red-blooded cells in her body appreciated the sight of a healthy, well-built man like Marc walking away.

His broad shoulders and wide back stretched the material of his expensive white dress shirt as he moved. Dark gray slacks that probably cost more than she made at the bakery in a week hugged his hips, and more importantly, his butt. A very nice, well-rounded butt that didn't seem to have changed much since they'd been together.

Lifting a hand to her face, she covered her eyes and silently chastised herself for being so weak-willed. What was wrong with her? Was she crazy? Or catching a bug? Or were her hormones still dreadfully out of whack because of the pregnancy?

Spreading her fingers a few brief centimeters, she peeked through and knew exactly what her problem was.

Number one—she knew what lay beneath all that cotton and wool. She knew the strength of his muscles, the texture of his skin. She knew how he moved and how he smelled and how he felt pressed up against her.

Number two—her hormones probably *were* out of whack— and not just the pregnancy variety. The regular ones seemed to be turned all upside down, as well.

Which was no surprise. She'd always been a total pushover where Marc was concerned. One smoldering look and her bones had turned to jelly. One brush of his knuckles across her cheek or light touch of his lips on hers and she'd been putty in his hands.

Given how long it had been since they'd been together— how long it had been since she'd been anything more than a human incubator and a first-time mommy—it was no wonder, really, that her mind was wandering down all sorts of deliciously naughty garden paths.

And no doubt if Marc knew, or even suspected, he would take full advantage of her vulnerability and inner turmoil, so it would be wise of her not to do or say anything to give him the wrong idea. Or any ideas at all, for that matter.

Through her fingers, Vanessa watched him undo the top couple of buttons of his shirt and loosen his collar. Such a familiar habit. She remembered him doing the same thing almost every night when he got home from work. He would usually spend a couple of hours in his home office, but taking off his jacket and tie, loosening his collar and rolling up his sleeves were the first steps toward relaxing for the evening.

She lowered her hands from her face just before he picked up the laptop and turned back around. Crossing the room, he lowered himself to the edge of the bed, set the laptop beside him, and then patted the pristine white coverlet.

"Come sit down for a minute," he said, "I want to show you something."

Vanessa raised a brow. "That sounds like another bad pickup line," she told him.

Marc chuckled. "Since when did you become so cynical? Now, come here so I can show you some of these plans I worked up for The Sugar Shack."

That got her attention, allaying some of her suspicions and fears—and giving rise to new ones. Moving to the bed, she sat down, tucking the skirt of her dress beneath her to keep from flashing too much leg.

He clicked a couple of buttons, then turned the screen so she could see it more easily. "You said you want to expand into the store space next door, right? Use it for a possible mail-order division of the business."

"Mmm-hmm."

"Well, this is a quick prospectus I worked up before dinner for what I think it would cost to renovate the space, what your expenses and overhead would be, et cetera. Of course, there are a lot of aspects to the bakery business I'm sure I'm not familiar with, so it will need to be adjusted. But this gives us a rough estimate and an idea of where to start."

He got up for a second and stretched to reach the bureau,

grabbing a large yellow legal pad before returning to the bed, sending the mattress bouncing slightly.

"And this is a rudimentary sketch of a possible layout for the expansion. Counters and shelving and such."

She pulled her attention away from the document on the computer screen to the tablet he was holding out to her. She studied the drawing for a minute, picturing everything exactly as it would look next door to The Sugar Shack.

It was good. Encouraging, even. And the idea that something so simple might one day soon be a reality caused her heart to leap in her chest.

There was only one problem.

Lifting her head, she met Marc's gaze. "Why did you do all this?" she asked, passing the legal pad back to him.

"Nothing is written in stone," he murmured, setting aside the tablet and turning the laptop back toward him. "And it won't be cheap, believe me. But the expansion is a good idea. I think it's a smart move and has the potential to really pay off in the long run. Especially if you do well enough to start that Cookie-of-the-Month Club thing you mentioned."

Her heart jumped again, making her palms damp and her throat tight. It was so nice to hear someone sharing her enthusiasm about branching out with the bakery and actually supporting her ideas.

But in this case, there were strings attached. So many strings.

"That doesn't answer my question," she said softly. And then she asked again, even though a part of her was afraid of his response. "Why did *you* do all this?"

He sat back, clicking the lid of the laptop closed and moving the computer to the nightstand, along with the legal pad.

"You need a partner to pull this off, Vanessa. You know

that, or you wouldn't have gone to Blake and Fetzer for help."

Her pulse slowed and the temperature in the room fell ten degrees. Or maybe it was only her own internal temperature that dropped like a stone.

"I told you, Marc, I won't take your money."

Shoulders going back, his spine straightened almost imperceptibly, and his jaw went square and tight. A clear indication he was about to get stubborn and lay down the Law According to Marc Keller.

Mouth a thin, flat line, he said, "And I told you, Vanessa, that I'm not going anywhere. Not for a while, anyway."

A beat passed while the tension seemed to leak from his stiff form and jump across the bed into her. The last thing she needed was a reminder of Marc's refusal to leave town now that he knew about Danny, and all the fears and concerns his presence brought to the surface.

"So as long as I'm sticking around," he continued, "we might as well use the time wisely. Why not get started on the expansion and put you one step closer to your goal?"

Oh, he was smooth and made so much sense. She'd always hated that, because it put him entirely too close to being right.

Of course, he usually *was* right, at least where business issues were concerned, which was even more annoying. Especially since he knew it and often came across as just this side of smug in that awareness.

"I don't want your help, Marc."

Rising from the bed, she linked her arms around her middle and paced across the room. When she hit the closed door, she turned and paced back, keeping her gaze locked on the worn and faded carpeting beneath her feet.

"I don't want to be tied to you, to owe you for anything."

"Well, it's a little late for that, don't you think?"

She stopped, lifted her head to meet his eye. One dark brow was raised, his lips curled in a wry half smile.

"We have a child together. I'd say that ties us together more strongly than any business plan or partnership ever could."

She blinked. Dammit. There it was again. He was right and being smug about it.

For better or worse, they *were* tied to each other now until the end of time through their son. Birthdays, school events, extracurricular activities, chicken pox, measles, puberty, girlfriends, his first tattoo or piercing...

She shuddered. Oh, God, please no piercings or tattoos. That might actually be the one parental matter she'd happily delegate to Marc for a good old-fashioned father-to-son heart-to-heart.

But given how ugly and heartbreaking—at least on her part—their separation had been, it was no wonder she wasn't looking forward to sharing any of that with him. And no wonder she'd tried to keep Danny a secret to begin with. It might not have been the right thing to do, but it sure made life a lot less complicated.

"That's different," she said quietly.

He inclined his head, though whether in agreement or simply acquiescence, she wasn't sure.

"However you feel about that," he said slowly, "it doesn't change the facts. I'm going to be in Summerville, getting to know my son and make up for lost time, for several weeks, at least. You might as well take advantage of that—and of my willingness to invest money into your bakery."

Pushing up from the bed, he came to stand in front of her, cupping his hands over her shoulders. His slightly callused palms felt rough against her bare skin, his warmth seeping into her pores.

"Think about it, Nessa," he murmured barely above a whisper. His eyes, as green and lush as summer moss, bored into hers. "Use your head here instead of sticking to stubborn pride. The smart and savvy businesswoman in you knows I'm right, knows this is an opportunity you'd be crazy to pass up. Even if it is coming from your despicable ex-husband."

He said the last with a quick wink and a self-deprecating quirk of his full, sexy lips.

It was that wink and the fact that he knew how badly she *didn't* want him around but apparently wasn't holding it against her that made her stop and think, just as he'd suggested.

Think through his offer logically and reasonably, and with the level-headed, straightforward intelligence that had convinced her to take the risky financial plunge of opening The Sugar Shack with Aunt Helen in the first place. Weigh her options. Weigh her desire to expand the bakery and accept a much-needed infusion of cash and support against her desire to keep Danny to herself, keep miles upon miles of distance between her and Marc—both figuratively and literally—and maintain complete control over her business rather than sharing it with a third party who may or may not be as genuinely committed to its growth and success as she and her aunt were. Or worse yet, had the power to crush her and her business at the slightest provocation.

And there would be provocation, wouldn't there? There already was, in that she'd kept first her pregnancy and then Danny's existence from him to begin with.

For all she knew, he could be hiding his true feelings from her, being kind and considerate and generous in an effort to lull her into a false sense of security. Then the minute she agreed to take his money, to let him partner with her in the bakery and to be a part of Danny's life, he would spring the trap, taking *everything* from her.

Her business, her security, her *son*.

Did she really believe that, though? Despite the bitterness

involved on both sides of their divorce, he had never been deliberately cruel. He hadn't tried to hurt her, hadn't used his powerful influence or family fortune to leave her destitute.

Thanks to the prenuptial agreement his family—or more to the point, his mother—had insisted on before their wedding, Vanessa had left the marriage with not much more than she'd walked into it with, but she was well aware that it could have been worse.

She had friends who had gone through much nastier divorces. She'd heard the horror stories where women who had been married to extremely wealthy men were put through the wringer and kicked onto the street with barely the clothes on their backs, sometimes with their children in tow.

Marc had never been that type of man. He'd always had a very low-key personality, opting for silent fury over angry blow-ups.

Even during their marriage, he might not have been as attentive as she would have liked or taken her complaints about his family or his distance seriously, but he had never resorted to petty arguments or name-calling. A couple of times, she'd even wished for something like that, if only as proof that he still cared enough to fight. With her or for her; back then, either would have translated as caring *at all*.

But his response to marital conflict had always been to lock his jaw, slip into stony silence and go back to the office to work even longer hours that pushed them even farther apart.

Marc was also one of the most honest men she'd ever met. It would be just like him to compartmentalize their current relationship.

Anything involving Danny would remain strictly personal, and he would deal with her on a personal, father-to-mother level. Anything involving her bakery would remain strictly a business venture and he would treat it as such.

If he pulled out of The Sugar Shack, it would be only his money and professional ties that went with him, not his love for Danny or determination to be in his son's life. And on the other side of the coin, if they were at odds about something that concerned Danny, he would never pull his financial backing of the bakery just to make her life miserable.

Unfortunately, she'd never been quite as good at keeping her work and her personal life separated. She loved The Sugar Shack. It was a part of her, built of blood, sweat, tears and most of all, heart. If it failed, if something happened to it or she had to close the doors, a very big part of her would die with it.

But even more important than that, and definitely what owned a much bigger portion of her heart and soul, was Danny. She would light a match and torch The Sugar Shack down to the ground if it meant keeping her child happy and safe.

And for better or worse, Marc was Danny's father, a part of him. He was also probably the only investor she would ever find who was actually willing and able to give the bakery an influx of much-needed cash, and who apparently thought her ideas for expansion held actual merit.

Anyone else would have already jumped at the offer. But there was so much at stake for her—and for Danny and Aunt Helen.

She'd been silent for so long, she was surprised Marc didn't check her for a pulse. She also suspected she would have the mother of all headaches soon just from the strain of thinking so hard. It was as though a Ping-Pong championship tournament was taking place inside her brain.

But in the end, she didn't follow her head or even her heart. She followed her gut.

"All right," she told him, the words nearly torn from a throat gone tight with the strain of her internal struggle. "But

I don't want your charity. If we're going to do this, then I want it to be completely official and aboveboard. We'll have Brian draw up investment papers, or make it a legal loan that I *will* pay back, or however these things are normally done."

Marc smiled gently, the sort of smile a parent offers a recalcitrant child, almost as though he was getting ready to humor her.

"Fine. I'll call Brian in the morning and get the ball rolling."

She nodded slowly, still reluctant, still unsure. Gut or no gut, agreeing to let Marc become a partner in her and her aunt's business still made her hugely uncomfortable, and there was no guarantee that it wasn't a monumental mistake.

"So that's the business end of things. We'll iron out the details tomorrow," he said. Then he ran his hands down the bare flesh of her arms from her shoulders to her elbows and lowered his voice to a near whisper. "Now on to something a bit more personal."

Her first thought was that he wanted to discuss Danny again, and her heart dropped all the way to her stomach, only to jump back up and lodge in her throat. Her chest grew tight as she held her breath and waited—for the bomb to drop, for him to demand full custody or announce that he was taking their son back to Pittsburgh with him.

Instead, he tugged her close, lowered his head and kissed her.

Seven

For a moment, Vanessa stood completely frozen, eyes wide, shock holding her immobile. But then his heat, his passion, seeped into her, and she began to lean against him, his eyes sliding closed on a silent sigh.

Marc's hands slipped from her elbows to her waist, pulling her even more tightly to him and holding her there with his arms crossed like iron bands at her back. His lips were warm and firm and masterful, plundering even as he attempted to coax and seduce.

He tasted like coffee and cream, and felt like heaven. Just as she remembered.

Kissing Marc had always been pure pleasure, like a cool glass of water on a hot summer day or sinking into a relaxing bubble bath after a long, exhausting day at work.

Hand drifting up to cup her cheek, Marc pulled away just enough to let her catch her breath and meet his gaze. His eyes were dark with a desire that Vanessa knew must be reflected in her own. Whether she wanted it or not, whether she liked it or not, there was no denying the heat that flared between them. Even now, after a year of separation, after the end of their marriage.

"I've been wanting to do that all evening," Marc murmured, his thumb slowly stroking just beneath her lower lip.

She wished she could deny feeling the same way, but had to admit that the thought of kissing him again had crossed her mind a few times since their unexpected reunion, as well. Especially during dinner, while they'd stared at one another across the candlelit table.

But kissing him wasn't a good idea. Being alone with him in his hotel room for much longer wasn't a good idea.

She should leave. Put a hand to his chest, push him away and get out while she could still make her legs move.

His other hand came up to frame her face, his fingers running through the hair at her temple.

Move, legs, move.

But her legs didn't move. It was as though her entire body had turned to stone, every muscle statue-still.

"This is a bad idea," she told him, putting her thoughts into words and forcing them past stiff, dry lips. "I should go."

A hint of a grin played at the corners of his lips. "Or you could stay," he whispered, "and we can see about turning a bad idea into a good one."

Inside, she was shaking her head. *No, no, no.* Sticking around was only going to turn the bad that had already happened into much, much worse.

No, she needed to leave. And she would, just as soon as she could get her body to obey the commands of her brain.

But the connection between the two had obviously been blocked or severed or scrambled in some way. Because she didn't move. She didn't step back, or push him away, or voice further arguments against making any more monumental mistakes.

She simply stood there and watched his mouth descend once again. Stood there and let his lips cover hers, let his fingers dig into her hair and cradle her scalp. Let his tongue tease and taunt until she had no choice but to open her mouth and invite him inside.

Oh, this is a bad idea, she thought, as her own arms came up to wind around his neck, her fingers toying with the hair at his nape. *A very, very bad...*

His tongue twined with hers and she groaned, any semblance of rational thought flying right out the window. Good or bad, she was in it now, with very little might left to fight. She wasn't even sure she wanted to anymore.

Though they were already touching, he tugged her even closer, so that her breasts flattened against his chest and the evidence of his arousal pressed between her legs.

Being a woman kept her arousal from being as obvious, but it was there, without a doubt. Besides the fact that her heart was pounding and her temperature was slowly reaching the boiling point, inside the cups of her bra her nipples were turning into tight, sensitive pearls. Lower, her knees were weak and her panties were growing damp.

It wouldn't take much more of Marc's intense ministrations for him to know just how aroused she was, too. Already, his hands were wandering down her sides and over her hips, his fingers slowly rucking up the skirt of her dress until he could touch her stockinged thighs.

Her own fingers went to the buttons at the front of his shirt, slipping one after another through their holes. When she reached the bottom, she switched to unbuckling his belt and loosening the top button of his dress slacks, then tugging the shirt's tail free. Once both sides fell open, she slipped her hands under the expensive material and put her palms flat against the warm, smooth skin of his chest and stomach.

He groaned. She moaned. The sounds met and mingled, sending shivers from their locked lips all the way down her spine.

As though he felt them, too, Marc's hand went to the small of her back and followed the line of her vertebrae up, up, up. He kneaded her neck a short second before catching the clasp of her dress's zipper and tugging it down in one long *ziiiiiiiiip* of sensation.

Curling her nails into his chest, she slumped into him as wave after wave of longing rolled through her. It was almost too much to bear, melting her bones and stealing the breath from her lungs. If he hadn't been holding her, she was sure she would have collapsed to the ground in a pile of skin and rumpled red fabric.

He released her mouth, allowing her to suck in some much-needed oxygen while he tugged at her dress, letting the flowy fabric pool at her feet. Hooking his thumbs into the waist of her pantyhose, he started to skim them down her legs, following them until he knelt in front of her on one knee.

With a hand at her ankle, he said, "Lift."

She did, and he slipped both her matching red heel and the stockings off her foot.

"Lift," he said again, repeating the motion on her other ankle, leaving her standing in the middle of the room in nothing but her bra and panties.

Thank goodness she'd taken as much care choosing those as she had her dress and shoes. She'd had absolutely no notion and no intention of letting him get so much of a glimpse of her underthings, but now she was infinitely relieved that she'd made a point of wearing a brand-new matching set. A strapless red demi-bra with scalloped lace edging and lacey, boy-cut panties that covered more than enough in the front, but left half moons of bare flesh visible from the back.

From his position on the floor, Marc must have noticed the peekaboo style of the underwear, because he lifted his head and shot her a grin that could only be described as wolfish.

"Lovely," he murmured, his hands cupping the backs of her calves, then her knees, then her thighs until her thighs quivered and she wasn't sure she could remain upright much longer.

Her tongue darted out, licking dry lips. "Mothers always tell their children to wear nice underwear, just in case," she managed in a shaky voice. "Now I know why."

Marc chuckled. A low, sexy sound that beat at her insides like tiny orange flames.

"These are better than nice," he told her, cupping her bottom and pressing a kiss to the bare skin of her belly, just below her navel. "But I'm pretty sure this isn't the kind of 'just in case' they're talking about."

A noise rolled up her throat that was meant to be a laugh. It came out more of a strangled hiss.

"But you like them, right? Better than plain white cotton?"

Kissing a line up the center of her torso, he climbed slowly to his feet. "Better than white cotton," he agreed. Then when he got to her mouth, he added, "But I don't really care, since you won't be wearing them much longer."

Reaching around her back, he unhooked her bra in one quick, deft movement. Only the last-minute crossing of her arms kept the garment from falling away completely.

"Now take them off. Both of them."

The gruff order sent her stomach flip-flopping and brought goose bumps to every inch of her exposed flesh. Which, considering her state of undress, was a considerable amount.

Despite the desire coursing through her veins, however, she suddenly felt awkward and exposed. She'd come this far, even knowing it was a colossal mistake.

It wasn't wise to be alone in the same room with Marc fully clothed, let alone do what they were doing. But being with him again brought back so many incredible memories and sensory perceptions that she'd thought she would never experience again. So she'd thrown up a thick, tall wall in her brain to keep right from wrong apart. And another between her brain and her heart to keep them from playing tug-of-war while she was enjoying Marc's kisses and touch. Now here she stood, half-naked, her ex-husband telling her to drop the two tiny bits of lace and fabric that kept her from being totally naked, and her nerves were calling foul.

For a brief moment, she considered jumping back into her dress and running for the hills. But that nice, thick wall was still firmly in place, leaving just enough want to overshadow future regrets.

What she needed, she realized, was a more level playing field.

Arms still crossed over her breasts to hold her bra in place, she stepped back. Just one small step away from him.

"Not yet," she told him, the words coming out more confidently than she felt.

He arched one dark brow and the message in his eyes clearly telegraphed that if she tried to cut and run, he would chase after her.

But she had no intention of running, only of evening things out a bit so that she wasn't the only one suffering a chill from the hotel's drafty old windows.

"You're overdressed," she pointed out. "So you first."

His right brow rose to meet the left and a muscle began to twitch along his jaw. Lifting his arms to waist height, he unbuttoned one cuff, then the other. With a roll of his broad shoulders, he shrugged out of the shirt completely, letting the pristine white material float to the floor behind him.

Vanessa swallowed. Making him strip down to next to nothing had seemed like a good idea at the time, but now that his chest was bare, she wasn't so sure. The very sight of that flat stomach and those tight pectorals had her mouth going desert dry and her heartbeat fluttering in her throat like the wings of a butterfly.

Without giving her time to regroup or even brace herself for more, he moved his hands to the front of his slacks and slowly lowered the zipper. Kicking off his shoes, he let the pants drop and stepped away from the entire pile—away from the clothes and one step closer to her.

"Better?" he asked, barely a foot of space separating them while the corners of his mouth curved in predatory amusement.

Not better. Definitely not better. If possible, it was worse. Because now, in addition to feeling anxious and exposed, she was also feeling extremely overwhelmed.

How could she have forgotten what this man looked like naked? Or nearly naked, at any rate.

There were male models out there being used for Calvin Klein and Abercrombie & Fitch ad campaigns who couldn't hold a candle to a fully dressed Marc. Undressed, in only his underwear, he blew them out of the water.

Out of his underwear...well, out of his underwear, he could blow water out of the water. No one would ever ask him to be a spokesperson for designer clothing or cologne, though, because putting him on billboards would cause women everywhere to swoon on the spot. They would cause traffic accidents and hit their heads on the pavement, and those were just lawsuits waiting to happen.

When they'd been married, Marc's good looks had amused her. The fact that he turned heads and invited so much female attention hadn't bothered her in the least, because she knew that at the end of the day, he was all hers. Other women could look, but she was the only one who got to touch.

They'd been divorced for over a year, though. How many other women had gotten to touch him in that time? How many heads had he turned who'd also managed to turn his?

As though sensing the direction of her thoughts, he lifted a hand to stroke her cheek. "Cold feet?" he asked quietly.

She shook her head in denial, but inside she was thinking, *Cold everything.*

She'd left him, been the one to initiate the divorce in the first place, but even so, she didn't want to think about him being with other women. It left her more than cold; it left her shaken.

Closing the space between them, he carefully pried her arms away from her breasts, but used his own chest to hold the bra in place. He ran his hands down the insides of her arms, then linked their fingers together. Just the way he used to, the way that used to make her feel so close to him, so cherished.

Pressing his lips to hers, he whispered, "Let me warm you up." Then he kissed her and started backing her slowly toward the bed.

The backs of her thighs hit the edge of the mattress and she toppled over, but Marc followed her down, so smoothly, it felt almost choreographed. The movement finally dislodged her bra and he grabbed it by one of the cups, tossing it aside.

His chest pressed her breasts flat and abraded the tight peaks of her nipples. She moaned, wrapping her arms around his shoulders while he kissed all but about three functioning brain cells straight out of her head.

Shifting his hands to her hips, he hooked his thumbs into the waist of her panties and dragged them down. He lifted her just enough to slip them off, then quickly shed his own.

They were both blessedly naked, pressed together like layers of cellophane. Insecurities threatened to surface again, reminding her that it had been months upon months since they'd been together…that she'd gone through a pregnancy and childbirth since then…that she'd spent her first trimester in a deep depression over the breakup of her marriage and the prospect of being a single mother—and therefore had spent a good deal of time in bed with cartons of ice cream and cookie dough that never quite made it into the oven.

In addition to baby weight, she'd put on pity-party weight, and though she'd been much more disciplined since she'd stopped feeling sorry for herself, she still hadn't managed to shed all of those extra pounds. Her hips were wider than before, her stomach far from flat, her thighs a bit more well-rounded.

The only upside to her new, more curvaceous figure was her bosom. Whether it was due to the pre-baby caloric binges or the post-baby breast-feeding, the increased bra size was kind of nice. And being bigger up top helped to keep the rest of her body in proper proportion.

But whether her recent physical changes were good or bad, Marc didn't seem to mind either way. In fact, he didn't even seem to notice. Or if he did, he was enjoying them enough that he didn't feel the need to comment.

Knowing that allowed Vanessa to relax and stop obsessing. Marc's hands on her body, his mouth trailing along her jaw, her throat, her shoulder, her collarbone, were too potent to ignore for long, anyway. As was the need to touch him in return.

She stroked his back, toyed with the hair at the nape of his neck. Nibbled his ear and rubbed her cheek against the slight stubble that was growing in and would need to be shaved clean again in the morning.

His erection was pressed between them, rubbing in

tantalizing places and she arched slightly to feel even more of that rigid length against her belly and lower. With a low growl, Marc sank his teeth into the muscle that ran from the side of her throat to her shoulder. She sucked in a sharp breath, groaning at the light stab of pleasure-pain and digging her nails into the flesh of his back to repay the favor.

He chuckled against her skin and she felt the vibrations clear down to her bones.

"Stop teasing," she ordered more than a little breathlessly just above his ear.

"You started it," he retorted, words muffled as he spoke into her skin. He trailed wet, openmouthed kisses across her chest, over the mound of one breast, tighter and tighter around her nipple.

"Besides, I'm not finished yet," he added a moment before taking that nipple into his mouth and suckling gently.

Oh, mercy. Vanessa's upper body shot off the mattress, pleasure streaking through her like lightning. She couldn't even cry out, the oxygen was knocked so thoroughly from her lungs.

She clung to his shoulders, panting and writhing as he didn't just tease, but tortured. He licked and nipped and sucked at one breast before moving to the other and driving her crazy all over again.

When he finished, he lifted his head and smiled down at her. A wicked, devilish smile.

He started to lean down and she was afraid of what he might do. She wasn't sure she could take much more, whether he decided to continue his cruel ministrations to her breasts or to move lower.

Oh, no, he couldn't go lower. Another time, maybe. Another time, she was sure she would be delighted, and more than willing to reciprocate.

But tonight, it would be too much. She couldn't bear it.

So before he got any bright ideas, she linked her legs around his hips and reached between them to take him in a firm, but careful grasp. He let out a hiss of breath, lips pulling back from his teeth and his eyes falling closed.

"Enough," she told him.

His lashes fluttered and he gazed down at her. "Do you want me to stop?" he murmured.

The bastard. He knew she didn't want him to stop, he was just teasing her—*torturing* her—again.

Giving him a little taste of his own medicine, she tightened her fingers around his arousal, causing him to gasp and flex his hips.

"Not stop-stop," she clarified, as though there were really any doubt, "just wrap up the opening act and get to the big bang already."

He arched a brow, his lips splitting into a wide grin. "The 'big bang,' huh?"

She felt her cheeks heat at her choice of words. Then again, she was lying naked beneath her ex-husband, all but done with the dirty deed, as it were. Was there really any reason to be embarrassed about *anything* at this point?

Taking a deep breath and pulling her chin up a notch, she said, "You heard me."

"Well," he replied slowly, that same predatory gleam in his eyes, that same sly smile, curving his mouth, "I'll see what I can do to deliver."

It was her turn to arch a brow and adopt an overconfident expression. "You do that."

His grin widened a second before he swooped in to place a rough, hard kiss on her lips. Then he reached down to cover her hand with his. Slowly, he pried her fingers away from that most sensitive of body parts and raised her arm over her head, pinning it to the mattress.

Shifting, he settled more fully between her legs, the tip

of his erection nudging her opening. And then he slid home, slowly, carefully, his mouth still covering hers, absorbing the heartfelt moans his agonizing entry dragged from her throat.

She clutched at his hands, both of them, where they held her own flat to the mattress. And he squeezed back, groaning against her lips as his hips began to move.

Inch by inch, he filled her up, stretching muscles and tissue that had been too long unused. It didn't hurt, though. On the contrary, it felt amazingly, wonderfully perfect.

Like so many times in the past, she marveled at how well they fit together, how every part of her body seemed to be molded, sculpted, designed for every part of his body. Even with the physical changes she'd gone through over the past year, that hadn't altered.

Levering himself up on his elbows, he released her mouth, giving her the chance to bite her bottom lip and tilt her head back in growing ecstasy. He did the same, nostrils flaring as he pulled out, then drove back in, slowly at first and then faster and faster.

She lifted her own hips, meeting him thrust for thrust, letting the motion, the flesh-on-flesh sensations wash over her in ever-increasing waves. Her lungs burned, struggling for air while the rest of her body struggled for completion. Every part of her tingled, tightening in longing, in expectation.

She wanted—no, *needed*—what only Marc could give her. And while slow and steady might be good for some things, like marathons and piano lessons, that's not what she was interested in right now. She wanted hard and fast and now, now, now!

"Marc, please," she begged, wrapping her arms more securely around his neck before leaning up to nip his earlobe. Then she sank her teeth even harder into his shoulder.

His entire body shuddered from head to toe above her, his

hands grasping her waist and digging in. He pounded into her with even more force, making her cry out, making himself cry out.

Pressure built until she wanted to scream and then suddenly the dam burst. Pleasure spilled over her in a splash of heat and colorful sparks, like fireworks going off overhead.

She called his name and clung to him for dear life, absorbing the delicious impact of his final thrusts, and finally his full weight as he collapsed atop her with a long, low groan of satisfied completion.

Eight

"This was probably a bad idea," Vanessa murmured.

Marc had wondered how long it would take her to start in on her list of regrets.

They were lying side by side, flat on their backs on the lumpy, queen-size hotel room mattress. Vanessa had the sheets pulled up to her armpits, held in place over her ample breasts by both hands. He was a bit more relaxed, stretched out and letting the sheet fall where it would, low on his abdomen and across his hips.

But while he was obviously taking their minor indiscretion in stride, he couldn't disagree with her on the "bad idea" part. He wasn't sorry, since making love with Vanessa wasn't something he could ever regret or apologize for, but she was right that it hadn't been the smartest decision of his life.

He wasn't even sure what had possessed him to kiss her in the first place.

Maybe because he'd been thinking about it all night,

his eyes straying over and over again to her mouth and the luscious cleavage visible above the bodice of her siren-red sex goddess dress.

Maybe because he hadn't been able to get her out of his head since the moment he'd seen her again after such a long absence…and after pretty much determining that he would never see her again at all.

Or maybe because she was simply irresistible. For him, she always had been.

It almost didn't surprise him that they'd made a child together at the very moment that their marriage had been falling apart around them. Despite their differences and the problems that had plagued them there at the end, physical compatibility had never even made it onto the list. No matter how bad a day either of them might be having, no matter how big a fight they might have had, it never seemed to take them long to come back together and set the sheets on fire.

It was a relief to know that hadn't changed. They were no longer married, she'd hidden his son from him and neither of them had a very clear vision of what the future held, but at least he knew the passion was still there. More than passion—lust and longing and desire thick enough to land a 747 on.

His leg brushed against hers beneath the covers and a jolt of that passion times ten shot through him. She jerked away from him, letting him know in no uncertain terms that his current state of semi-arousal would definitely be going to waste.

"You're right," he said, agreeing with her earlier statement. "Probably wasn't the wisest thing to do. At least not under the current circumstances."

"There's the understatement of the century," she grumbled, rolling to the side of the bed and carefully sliding her bare legs out from under the top sheet.

She sat there for a minute, not moving, and Marc took

the opportunity to admire the short fall of her copper hair around her shoulders, the supple line of her spine, and the gentle curves of her torso from the back. She'd put on a bit of weight with the pregnancy, but it didn't take away from her attractiveness one damn bit.

If anything, it made her even more beautiful, filling her out with sensual, womanly curves in all the right places. He had certainly enjoyed exploring those curves with his hands and lips, feeling them so soft and gentle against his much harder naked length.

One corner of his mouth lifted in amusement, not only from the delectable view, but from the snarky tone of her voice. She'd always had such a way with words, and a way of delivering them that often delighted him.

It had annoyed the hell out of her when she'd been in a snit, telling him off, and would catch him grinning. Not because he wasn't listening or taking her seriously, but because he'd always loved watching her and listening to her—even when she was chewing him out.

The way she moved, pacing back and forth and waving her arms. The way her breasts rose and fell in agitation, following the cadence of her rant. What could he say…it turned him on. And nine times out of ten, their arguments had led to phenomenal make-up sex, so there was really no downside to riling her up a little more by letting her think he was laughing off her anger or upset.

In hindsight, he could see how that might have led to some of the problems that had prompted them to split. He'd never meant to deride her feelings or opinions on anything, he'd simply believed their relationship was secure enough that any differences or misunderstandings they had would blow over just as they had in the past.

How wrong he'd been. And he hadn't seen it coming until it was too late. Too damn late.

"It can't happen again," she said, still facing the other direction.

For a moment, he remained trapped in his head and thought she was talking about their divorce. That definitely couldn't happen again, and if he had it to do over, it might not have happened in the first place.

Then he realized she meant the sex. Tonight's unplanned, unexpected, but definitely not unsatisfying, indiscretion.

"Marc," she said when he didn't respond. Twisting slightly, she tilted her head until she could see him from the corner of her eye, then repeated more firmly, "This can't happen again."

Rolling to his side, he propped himself up on one elbow, letting silence fill the room while he studied her. After a minute or two, he murmured, "What do you want me to say, Vanessa? That I'm sorry we made love? That I don't hope we get the chance to do it again…frequently and with great enthusiasm?" He shrugged the shoulder that wasn't holding him up. "Sorry, but I'm not going to do that."

"What is wrong with you?" she charged, all but leaping from the bed, dragging the sheet along with her. It caught on the corners of the mattress, of course, but not before sliding from his hips and leaving him in the buff down to his ankles.

She turned, yanking at the cheap, industrial grade white cotton until it came free, pointedly ignoring his total nudity. With a huff, she yanked the quilted coverlet from the foot of the bed and tossed it over him, head and all. He chuckled, lowering it just in time to watch her wrap the sheet like a toga around her own naked form.

"We're divorced, Marcus," she pointed out, as though he weren't painfully aware of their current marital status. Or lack thereof.

She stormed around the room gathering her clothing, piece

by discarded piece. "Divorced couples aren't supposed to sleep together."

"Maybe not, but we both know it happens all the time." He waved a hand to encompass the rumpled bed and their current states of postcoital undress.

"Well, it shouldn't," she argued back, doing her best to hold up the sheet while she struggled into her underwear. "Besides, you hate me."

A beat passed while the air in the room sizzled with growing tension. "Says who?"

At the softly spoken question, Vanessa jerked to a halt and lifted her head to meet his gaze. The lower half of the sheet, which had been hiked up around her thighs while she fought with her panties, fell to the ground.

"Don't you?" she asked just as softly. "I mean, you do. I know you do. Or at least, you should. I didn't tell you I was pregnant. I didn't tell you about Danny."

His brows crossed and his mouth dipped down in a scowl at the reminder. He'd been working hard to forget that part of his reason for being in town. Or more to the point, had been willing to suspend his anger and feelings of betrayal long enough to partake of Vanessa's lovely body and enjoy the tactile sensations of having her in his arms and bed again after so long.

He took in her still half-naked form, wrapped like a Greek goddess in pristine white cotton. Sure, all of the reasons he *should* hate her were still there. And no doubt they had many issues to work out. But for some reason, at that moment, he just couldn't get his temper to flare.

"Here's a bit of advice," he told her, cocking a brow and trying not to let his frown slip up into a grin. "When someone has temporarily forgotten that they have a reason to be mad at you, it's probably better not to remind them."

"But you should be mad at me," she said quietly, holding

his gaze for a long, drawn out second before turning her back to him and continuing to dress.

Marc watched as she struggled with her bra, then let the sheet fall as she hooked the bit of lingerie behind her back. He watched the light play on the pale canvas of her skin and the smooth lines of her body as she moved.

Interesting, he thought, fighting the urge to drag her back to bed. She seemed to *want* him to be angry with her.

On the one hand, at least he knew she hadn't slept with him in an effort to cloud his mind and seduce him into forgetting that she tried to keep his son from him. On the other, she'd have been wise to do almost anything to stay on his good side at this point. To avoid acrimony, a possible custody battle or to keep him from simply picking up and taking Danny home with him, leaving her few options to get him back.

Granted, before today, he hadn't spoken with Vanessa in over a year, and the fact that she'd left him meant he probably hadn't understood her all that well to begin with. But the only explanation he could think of for why she'd remind him of what stood between them was that she *needed* something between them. A wall. A barrier.

If he hated her, he might not want to be with her again. If he hated her, he might get fed up and storm home to Pittsburgh—preferably without Danny.

Oh, they'd work out some sort of custody agreement. On that, he would insist. And he was sure Vanessa wouldn't argue too strongly against it, not now. Agreeing to let him see Danny on a regular basis or even let him take their son back to Pittsburgh for the occasional extended visit would be the lesser of two evils for her now.

But he'd been in big business long enough to know that when someone gave up something too easily, it was usually because they were trying to get or retain something even more important to them. His best guess was that Vanessa was trying to retain distance.

She'd wasted no time moving to Summerville the minute their divorce was final, and as far as he could tell, she'd been perfectly happy settling in with her aunt and making her mark on the small town through The Sugar Shack.

If Fate hadn't somehow intervened to bring him here himself, he never would have known where she'd relocated to or that she had a child. *His* child.

Oh, yes, she'd wanted distance then, and she wanted it now. And if she pissed him off—or kept him pissed off—then he'd be less likely to stick around for any length of time, wouldn't he?

Which only made him want to stick around more. He was contrary like that sometimes, a fact Vanessa was well aware of. She should have known that if he caught on to her little plan, he'd make a point of doing pretty much the exact opposite of what she wanted, just to vex her.

Of course, there was a good chance she didn't even realize she had a little plan. That she was running heavily on instinct, her current thoughts and actions more subconscious than anything else.

But it still intrigued him, and if he hadn't wanted to stick around before just to be close to the child he hadn't known existed, he certainly did now. He was even looking forward to it, considering the entertaining side benefits he'd recently discovered could be added to his stay.

Tossing back the covers, he moved to the edge of the bed and sat up. "Well, I'm sorry to disappoint you, but I don't hate you."

He pushed to his feet and walked toward her stark naked. Where she'd fought so hard to protect her modesty and stay covered, he didn't bother and wasn't the least bit self-conscious about his nudity.

When she saw him coming, she took a jerky step back, away from him, but he wasn't really after her. Bending at the waist, he scooped up the tangled ball of his pants and underwear.

"I'm not happy about what you did," he clarified, climbing into his clothes with slow, deliberate movements, "and I can't say that I don't harbor a bit of anger and resentment over it. Or that there won't be moments when that anger and resentment flare hotter than anything else."

He leaned down for his wrinkled shirt and shrugged it on, but didn't bother buttoning it, leaving his chest bare down the middle. "But we've covered that ground already. Keeping Danny from me—or the pregnancy to begin with—was wrong. That's time and an experience I can't get back. Now that I know I have a son, however, things are going to change. I *am* going to be involved in his life—and therefore in yours."

She was standing only about three feet from him, clutching that red dress to her breasts to cover as much of her front as she could. It was silly and useless, a bit like locking the barn door after the bull had already escaped, but Marc found her false sense of modesty oddly endearing.

"You should probably come to terms with that," he told her matter-of-factly. "The sooner, the better."

She simply stood there, staring at him. Her eyes sparkled like polished sapphires, but whether with fear or rage or mere confusion, he couldn't quite tell.

While he had her off balance—which was a nice switch, frankly, since she'd pretty much had him off balance from the moment he'd driven into town—he tossed another can of gasoline on the bonfire that just seemed to continue blazing between them.

"Here's something else you should probably take into

consideration," he said quietly, widening his stance and crossing his arms determinedly in front of him.

Vanessa didn't reply. Instead, she cocked her head, the tendons at the sides of her throat convulsing as she swallowed, waiting nervously for him to elaborate.

"We didn't use a condom, which means that you may even now get pregnant with our second child."

Nine

Oh, God.

Marc's words slammed into Vanessa's chest like a bullet, knocking the air from her lungs and making her literally stagger on her feet.

What had she been thinking? Bad enough she'd fallen into bed with her ex-husband faster than a star falls from the sky, but she'd completely forgotten about protection of any kind. It had never occurred to her to insist he use a condom, and since she was a new mother, still breast-feeding and with absolutely zero romantic prospects on the horizon, it hadn't been necessary for her to be on birth control.

She tried to do the math in her head, to figure out when her last period had been and when she was due again, but panic kept her thoughts in a tailspin.

And what about the breast-feeding? Wasn't it supposed to be harder to get pregnant while still nursing?

Dear God, please let that be true, because she couldn't even fathom the idea that she might actually be pregnant *again*, unexpectedly, unplanned and by her *former* husband. It was almost too horrifying to contemplate.

"I'm not," she said, as though saying it firmly and decisively enough would make it true.

Marc raised a dark, sardonic brow. "How can you be so sure."

"I'm just not," she insisted, tearing frantically at her dress until she got her feet inside and could yank it up. Never mind that it was open all the way to her bottom in the back because she couldn't raise the zipper without help. She would walk home with it hanging loose, if she had to, rather than ask him for one iota of assistance.

"And what were you thinking?" she charged, stamping a foot as she slipped it into a strappy red heel. "How could you do that—let *me* do that—without taking precautions?" She cast him an angry, accusatory glare. "I've never known you to be so irresponsible."

He shrugged, looking exponentially more casual and unconcerned than she was feeling at that particular moment. "What can I say? I was swept away by your beauty and passion, and the exhilaration of being with you again after such a long absence."

Pausing in the act of shoving on her other shoe, she tilted her head in his direction and gave a loud, unladylike snort. *"Please,"* she scoffed.

"Is that so hard to believe?" he asked, still wearing the blank mask that gave her no clue of his true emotions.

Was he upset that they'd forgotten to use protection? Happy? Angry? Excited? Confused? Nauseous?

Because she was nauseous. And upset and angry and confused. There was no happiness or excitement anywhere on her radar.

If it turned out she really was pregnant…oh, God, please

don't let her be pregnant again—not by Marc, and not so soon after Danny's birth…she would of course love the baby. Unconditionally and without question. But the difference between loving an existing child and loving the notion of carrying an as-yet imaginary one—especially under these circumstances—was like the difference between black and white, hot and cold, thirsty and drowning.

She loved Danny with all her heart and soul. She wouldn't trade him for anything, or even go back and undo the events that had led to his birth.

But she sure as *hell* wouldn't choose to be pregnant again. Not so soon after having one child, not without benefit of marriage, and not with a man she'd so recently divorced.

She was already linked too closely to Marc, thanks to his discovery of Danny's existence. But the thought of being even more closely connected to him through a second child would be a nightmare come to life.

He was almost foaming-at-the-mouth rabid about staying close to her now that he knew about Danny. Having him know from the very beginning that he was going to be a father a second time would turn him into near-stalker material. She would never get rid of him, not even for short amounts of time while he commuted back and forth between Pittsburgh and Summerville.

Oh, no, knowing Marc, he would do something ridiculous like move to Summerville himself, or insist they get remarried and then drag her back to the city where she would be trapped and miserable all over again.

No, no, no, no, no. Vanessa's head was shaking like a tambourine as she ran her gaze around the room, looking for anything she might have forgotten. Her purse, her watch, an earring…

"I think you underestimate your appeal," Marc remarked,

apparently missing the nuclear meltdown taking place inside her.

Small red clutch in hand, she shot him another withering glare before spinning on her heel and marching toward the hotel room door.

"Vanessa."

Her free hand was out, reaching for the knob, but his sharp voice stopped her in her tracks. She didn't turn to look at him, but remained still, waiting for him to continue.

"I'll see you at the bakery first thing tomorrow, eight o'clock sharp. Be sure Danny is with you."

A shudder rolled through her, and she wasn't sure if it was aversion to having to deal with him again in the morning or relief that that was his only parting remark.

With a jerky nod, she pulled the door open and started to step into the hall.

"And I'll want to know as soon as you do," he went on, stopping her a second time.

Her heart lurched in her chest. "Know what?" she asked, forcing the words past her tight, dry throat.

"Whether or not we'll be presenting our son with a little brother or sister nine months from now."

Marc wasn't at The Sugar Shack when she and Aunt Helen arrived with Danny in tow at five o'clock the next morning. Vanessa wasn't surprised, since he'd said he would meet her there at eight, and frankly, she could use the short reprieve.

It might only be three hours, but it was three hours without having to see or deal with Marc. And after last night, she needed them. Desperately.

While she and Aunt Helen bustled around readying the bakery for the breakfast opening, she tried her best to put him and the myriad of issues between them out of her mind. Not for the first time…not even for the five hundred and first time…she wondered how she'd managed to get herself into such an incredible mess.

It felt as though her life had turned into some kind of daytime soap opera, and the worst part was that she knew those things were never-ending. They just went on forever, with more and more dramatic cliff-hangers cropping up to throw the main characters into a tizzy.

Well, she didn't need any more tizzies. And she sure as heck didn't need any more drama. If she could have, she'd have canceled her own personal variation of *As the World Spins Out of Control.*

Unfortunately, those few hours of blessed freedom sped by much too quickly. Before she knew it, Summerville's early risers were filing in for a morning coffee and croissant on their way to work, or to sit and enjoy a more leisurely sticky bun with a cup of hot tea. Even before the clock struck eight o'clock, her eyes were practically glued to the front door, waiting for Marc to arrive.

But the clock did strike eight and he didn't appear. Then it struck ten after, twenty after, quarter to nine, and he was still nowhere in sight.

She should have been relieved, but instead, Vanessa found herself beginning to worry. It wasn't like Marc to be late for anything, especially after making such a production of warning her of where he would be when—and where he fully expected her to be to meet him.

She rang up an order for four coffees and a box of mixed Danish pastries with one eye on the time, trying to decide if she should bask in her apparent—and most likely fleeting—freedom, or call the Harbor Inn to check on him.

By nine-thirty, she'd not only decided to call the hotel, but if he wasn't there, intended to drive over herself to search his room, and call the police, if necessary. But before she could untie her apron and ask Aunt Helen to cover the front counter for her, the bell above the door rang and Marc strolled in, a charming smile on his face.

As hard as she tried not to notice, he looked magnificent. In place of his usual suit and tie, he wore tan slacks and a light blue chambray shirt. The shirt's collar was open, cuffs rolled up to midforearm.

Anyone else might see Marc and think he was just a run-of-the-mill guy, out and about on a beautiful summer day. But Vanessa knew better. If one looked closer, one would notice the solid gold Rolex, the seven-hundred-dollar Ferragamo loafers and the air of absolute power and confidence that surrounded him.

This was Marc's casual appearance, but as wise men knew, appearances could be extremely deceptive.

He walked through the maze of small round tables as though he owned the place, his smile turning more and more predatory the closer he came to the tall glass display case that separated them.

"Good morning," he greeted, sounding much too chipper for her peace of mind.

"Morning," she returned with much less enthusiasm. "You're late. I thought you said you'd be here at eight."

One solid shoulder rose and fell in a casual shrug. "I had some errands to run."

She raised a brow, but didn't ask because she wasn't sure she wanted to know.

"Do you have a minute?" he asked.

She glanced around, judging the number of customers at the tables and the few people who were milling in front of the display case, trying to decide which sweet was most worth ruining their diets.

With a quick nod, she moved toward the kitchen and dipped her head through the swinging double doors. "Aunt

Helen, could you work the register for a second? I need to speak with Marc."

Aunt Helen finished what she was doing and came out, wiping her hands on the front of her apron while Vanessa removed hers and hung it on a small hook on the far wall. Her aunt cast Marc a cautious, almost disparaging glance, but held her tongue, thank goodness.

Vanessa hadn't told Aunt Helen what happened with Marc the night before. She'd given a brief recap of dinner, acting as though all they'd discussed was the bakery and a potential business agreement, and that everything had remained very professional. But she hadn't mentioned word one about following him up to his hotel room or letting things get out of control. And she certainly hadn't shared the fact that her hormones had so overwhelmed her common sense that she'd allowed Marc to make love to her without any form of doctor-recommended birth control.

Knowing the whole story would only have increased Aunt Helen's animosity toward Marc. There was a time, not so long ago, when Vanessa welcomed her aunt's protectiveness and having someone to talk to about everything she'd been through both before and during the divorce.

But things had changed now. Not necessarily for the better, but in ways she couldn't avoid. Marc knew about Danny, was determined to be a part of his son's life, and that meant he was going to be a part of hers. For better or worse, she had to find a way to make peace with her ex-husband, if only to keep the next eighteen years of her life from being a living hell.

In order to do that, and also keep the peace with her aunt, she had to avoid bad-mouthing Marc. She probably shouldn't have done so in the first place, but she'd been so hurt, so miserable, that she'd had to talk to *someone,* and Aunt Helen's had been the perfect shoulder to cry on.

Marc came up behind her, laying a hand gently on her elbow. As soon as she was sure Helen was settled behind the counter, she let him lead her across the bakery and through the shared entrance that led to the empty space next door.

She thought they were simply going to use the area to talk privately, and her stomach was nearly in knots wondering what sort of shoe or bomb or anvil he would drop on her this time. But rather than stopping in the center of the empty space, he kept walking, pulling her with him to the front of the building and the glass door that opened out onto the sidewalk.

"Do you have a key for this?" he asked, pointing to the door's lock.

"Yes. The landlord knows I'm interested in renting the space and occasionally lets me use it for small bits of storage. Plus, I can let other potential renters in if he isn't available."

"Good," he replied, his warm hand still cupping her elbow more intimately than she would have liked. "I'm going to need it."

She blinked. "Why?"

"To let those guys in," he answered, cocking his head in the direction of the glass and the street beyond. "Unless you want them traipsing through your bakery and dragging all their dirty, heavy equipment with them."

Following his gaze, she blinked again, only then noticing that the sidewalk outside the empty storefront was littered with men in jeans and work shirts unloading toolboxes, sawhorses, lumber and various cutting implements from the row of pickup trucks parked at the curb.

"Who are they?" she asked in dismay.

"Your construction crew."

She met Marc's gaze and must have looked as confused as she felt because he quickly elaborated.

"They're here to clean the place up and start putting in your shelving and countertops."

"What? Why?"

Her ex-husband's expression went from being amused at her utter shock to exasperated at her apparent denseness. "It's all part of the expansion plan, remember? We've got to get this section of the building renovated for The Sugar Shack's mail-order distribution and that Cookie of the Month thing you have in mind."

Her gaze swung from Marc to the workers outside, to Marc, to the workers… She now knew exactly how wild animals felt when caught in the middle of the highway by bright, oncoming headlights.

"I don't understand," she said with a slow shake of her head. "I didn't hire them. They can't start working here because I haven't rented the space yet. I don't have the money."

Marc gave a perturbed sigh. "Why do you think I'm here, Vanessa? Aside from wanting to spend time with Danny. Don't you remember what we discussed last night?"

She remembered last night. Vividly. And she remembered his parting shot that he hadn't used a condom, she hadn't been on the pill and she might very well be pregnant with his child. Again. The rest was a bit more of a blur, especially at this particular moment.

One of the workers came to the door. Marc made a motion with his hand, indicating that he needed a minute or two more, and the man nodded, returning to his truck.

"Look, it's taken care of, okay?" Marc told her. "I talked to the building's owner about the modifications we want to make. The space will be rented in your name, and part of the agreement will include permission to make any changes we see fit to better our business. Brian is putting together the paperwork and will deliver the contracts today. I'll have him get me a copy of the key from the landlord, but for now I need the one you have."

"But…" She was starting to sound like a broken record. "If Brian hasn't talked to Mr. Parsons yet, how do you know he'll agree to let us—*me*—rent this space?"

His mossy green eyes sparkled with self-assurance. "Vanessa," he said slowly, as though speaking to a small child or particularly slow adult. "It's taken care of. The building is for rent, I told Brian to rent it. What more do you need to know?"

She was finally catching on. Or rather, finally fully absorbing the situation and Marc's deep-rooted resolve to stay in town.

"Let me guess. 'Money is no object,'" she mimicked, adopting a low, masculine voice that was clearly supposed to be his. "You told Brian what you wanted—with no limit on how much you were willing to spend—and are leaving him to do whatever he has to for you to get your own way."

Releasing her elbow, he propped his hands on his hips, letting out a frustrated breath. "What's wrong with that?" he wanted to know.

She wished she could say nothing. She wished she didn't mind that he was using his wealth and prestige to assist her in her business and help to make the bakery an even bigger success.

There had even been a time when that sort of power and cocky confidence would have impressed her. Now, though, it only made her nervous.

"I don't want to be indebted to you, Marc," she told him softly, honestly. "I don't want to owe you anything, or know that The Sugar Shack has only expanded, is only successful, because you rode into town and saved the day with the Keller family fortune."

"Why does it matter where the capital comes from,

Vanessa? The important thing is that you're getting your additional space and branching out into mail order."

Shaking her head, she crossed her arms beneath her breasts and took a step back. "You don't understand. It *does* matter, because if you come in waving your checkbook around and running roughshod over me and everyone else in this town, then it's not *my* business anymore. It's just another insignificant acquisition for Keller Corp's multimillion-dollar holdings."

Widening his stance, he copied her defensive position of arms over chest. "Don't give me that. You asked Brian Blake to look for an investor you could work with. Preferably a silent one who would be willing to flush copious amounts of money into the bakery, but not have much say on how it was run or what you did with the cash. For the most part, that's exactly what I'm doing. So your problem isn't that I'm 'waving my checkbook around,' as you so eloquently put it. Your problem is that it's *my* checkbook."

"*Of course* that's my problem," she snapped, his earlier frustrations rubbing off on her. "We've been down this road before, Marc. The money, the influence, expecting everyone and everything to fall into line simply because your name is Keller."

Uncrossing her arms, she raised her hands to cover her face for a minute, trying to collect her thoughts and her temper. Once she lowered them, her tone was more subdued.

"Don't get me wrong, I liked it for a while. I enjoyed the lifestyle being your wife afforded me. The parties, the wardrobe, never having to worry about making ends meet."

Oh, yes. After a lifetime of struggling, of working her fingers to the bone just to get by, marrying into money had been a welcome reprieve.

"But you have no idea what it was like to be your wife and live under that roof without truly being a Keller."

His eyes narrowed, their green depths filling with genuine confusion. "What are you talking about? Of course, you were a true Keller. You were my wife."

"That's sure not how it felt," she admitted softly, remembering all the times his mother had made a point of reminding her that she was a Keller by marriage only, making her feel as though she had no business even crossing the threshold of Keller Manor without a mop and feather duster in her hands.

"I'm sorry." His arms slid from his chest and he started to reach for her, then seemed to think better of it and dropped his hands to his sides. "I never meant to make you feel like an outsider."

Guilt stabbed through her at the hurt look on his face. She opened her mouth to tell him that he hadn't been nearly as big an offender as his mother, but a sharp rap on the glass cut her off, startling them both.

The same worker as before, apparently the man in charge of the rest of the crew, made an impatient face and tapped his watch. Time, as they said, was money, and he obviously wasn't making any standing around on the sidewalk. Of course, Vanessa was sure Marc was paying them well, and most likely by the hour, regardless of whether they were actively working or not.

Marc lifted a hand, giving him the *just a second* gesture before turning back to her. "I'm going to need that key before these guys decide to sledgehammer their way in here."

She licked her lips and swallowed, reluctant to do his bidding. She and Marc had been on the verge of an honest-to-goodness adult conversation. One where she'd finally almost worked up the courage to tell him the truth behind why she'd gotten fed up and left in the first place. She'd tried so many times in the past to let him know how she was being treated, how much she felt like an outcast in what was supposed to be her own home, but she'd never quite been brave enough to blurt it out.

Part of her had believed that if he loved her enough, if he understood her as much as a husband was supposed to understand his wife, then he would know what she was trying to say all the times she'd hinted at her growing unhappiness. Now, she realized that nobody should be expected to be a mind reader, especially someone of the male persuasion.

If only she had been wise enough and gutsy enough to simply tell him what was going on. Things might have turned out so differently.

But that was water under the bridge and any chance they might have had of wiping the slate clean this morning had disappeared with the carpenter's untimely interruption.

Licking her lips again, she inclined her head. "I'll get the key," she said, turning on her heel and hurrying away.

Ten

"I swear, that racket is enough to make me want to jump into this oven myself."

Vanessa raised her head from the perfect circles of pastry dough she was currently topping with raisin filling to watch Aunt Helen slide a tray of baklava into one of the industrial ovens and slam the door with a clang that only punctuated the loud, staccato sounds of construction coming from the other side of the bakery walls.

It hadn't been easy to put up with both the noise and the added traffic of having so many workers around. She'd made dozens of apologies to customers, as well as creating *Please excuse our dust* and *Apologies for the excessive noise* signs. Thankfully, no real dust or debris had made it into the actual bakery side of the building, but having the crew around all day every day didn't make it easy for folks to come in and enjoy a *quiet* cup of tea and scones.

"They'll be finished soon," she told her aunt, repeating

the line the construction foreman had been giving her for the past week. She was familiar enough with this type of thing to know that "soon" was an extremely relative term, but given the fact that they really were making amazing progress, she thought the job would likely be done in just another week or two.

"And you have to admit, it's been nice of Marc to do all of this for us."

Aunt Helen gave a derisive snort. "Don't fool yourself, dear. He isn't doing it to be nice. He's doing it for himself, and to keep you under his thumb, and you know it."

Vanessa didn't respond, mostly because her aunt was right. Without a doubt, Marc wouldn't still be in town if there wasn't something in it for him.

He wanted to be close to Danny and indeed spent almost every evening at Aunt Helen's house with them. They ate dinner together. He helped feed Danny, gave him baths and put him to bed. At his insistence, she'd shown him how to change a diaper, and amazingly, he now did that almost as often as she did. They played on blankets on the floor, and took walks, and went to the park, even though Danny was too young to truly enjoy it.

It all felt so normal, and Vanessa had to admit…nice.

But just as Aunt Helen had reminded her, she couldn't forget for a minute that there were strings attached to everything Marc did. He wanted to know his son, which was understandable and seemed innocent enough on the surface.

Beyond that, though, she knew the entire situation was steeped in ulterior motives. Or at least the potential for ulterior motives.

Right now, Marc was using the remodeling and bakery expansion as an excuse to be close to his son, and something to occupy his time while Danny took frequent naps. But what would happen later?

What would happen once he decided he'd gotten to know Danny as well as he could here in Summerville and wanted to take him back to Pittsburgh to assume his rightful place on one of the silver-lined branches of the Keller family tree?

What would happen when the novelty of helping her create a mail-order business for The Sugar Shack wore off and small town living began to bore him?

And why did she bother wondering about such silly questions, when she already knew the answers?

The past couple of weeks, Marc had reminded her more of the man she'd fallen in love with and married than ever before. He'd been kind and generous, sweet and funny. He held doors for her, offered to help her clear the table after meals and put their son down for naps.

And he touched her. Nothing overt or overly sexual that a casual observer might notice, even considering how they'd spent his first night in town. Just a light brush of his fingers now and then—down her arm, over the back of her hand, along her cheek as he tucked a strand of hair behind her ear.

She tried not to read too much into the familiar gestures, but that didn't keep her pulse from thrumming or her heart from hammering inside her chest. Aunt Helen had complained more than once that the house or bakery was too cold, but turning up the air conditioning was the only way Vanessa could think of to combat the erratic spikes in her body temperature that Marc's constant presence and attentions created.

Speak of the devil.

No sooner had the memory played through her head than Marc pushed open the swinging kitchen doors, and she nearly bobbled the spoon she was using to dollop raisin filling onto the tray.

There went her temperature again, causing her skin to flush and perspiration to break out along her brow and between her breasts. At least this time, she could blame it on the ovens and all the hard work she was putting in trying to fill an order for six dozen raisin-filled cookies by three o'clock.

"When you get a minute," he said, "you should come over and see what you think. The crew is almost finished, and they want to know if there's anything else you'd like done before they go."

"Oh." That brought Vanessa's head up.

She'd been over to the other side of the shop a couple of times during the construction, but hadn't wanted to get in anyone's way. Plus, Marc had been so on top of things that her presence and input hadn't really seemed necessary.

But now that the renovations were nearly complete, she was suddenly excited to see how it looked. To start picturing herself there, boxing up her fresh-baked delights, overseeing the extra employees they would likely have to hire. Or would *get* to hire, if the mail-order idea was as successful as she hoped.

Sparing a glance at Aunt Helen, she dropped her spoon back in the bowl of lumpy, dark brown cookie filling, and began wiping her hands clean on a nearby towel.

"Do you mind?" she asked her aunt.

"Of course not. You go, dear," Aunt Helen told her, bustling over to take over with the cookies. "I'll just finish with these, and after you get back, maybe I'll take a peek at the new space myself."

Vanessa smiled and gave her aunt a peck on the cheek, then pulled off her apron and followed Marc. The occasional bit of sanding or hammering met her ears even before they reached the entryway between the two storefronts, but it had been going on for so long that it was nothing more than background noise now, and none of her regular customers seemed to notice or was bothered by it anymore.

Marc opened the door to the other side of the bakery and pushed back the sheet of thick plastic that had been hung as an extra precaution against sawdust and paint fumes. Holding it aside, he let her duck in ahead of him.

An awed sigh escaped her lips as she straightened and took in her nearly finished surroundings. The room was beautiful. More than she ever could have imagined, even after being in on the initial stages of planning.

Shelves and countertops of various sizes and heights lined the walls, creating more work space than she ever could have hoped for. The floor and ceiling had both been redone, and everything had been painted to match The Sugar Shack so that it was obviously an extension of the bakery itself.

"Oh!" Vanessa cried, putting her fingers to her lips.

"Does it meet with your approval?" Marc asked, amusement evident in his tone.

She was sure he could tell by her shaking hands and watery eyes just how pleased she was, but still she managed a breathless whisper, "It's wonderful."

Spinning around, she slowly took it all in again, and then again, her amazement growing with each turn. She didn't stop to think about how it had come about, the strings that were attached, or how costly the bill might be when it finally came due. All she knew was that this portion of the building was hers now, her chance to grow and expand the business of her heart.

With a tiny squeal of glee, she threw her arms around Marc's neck and squeezed him tight. Almost immediately, he circled her waist, hugging her back.

"Thank you," she whispered near his ear. "It's perfect."

When she pulled away, an odd expression crossed his face,

but before she could question it, the foreman appeared at her left shoulder. She was coming to think of him as the King of Rude and Untimely Interruptions.

"I take it she likes her new work area," he said with a smile, addressing Marc.

Considering that her arms were still linked around her ex-husband's neck, that wasn't a difficult observation to make. Feeling suddenly self-conscious, Vanessa cleared her throat and stepped back, putting a more respectable amount of distance between them.

"She does seem to like it," Marc replied.

"It's more than I ever could have hoped for," she told the two men. "Even after seeing the blueprints and design specs." She shook her head, sliding her hands into the pockets at the front of her white capris to keep from fidgeting. "I never imagined it would look this good."

"Glad you're happy. If there's anything else you need, or any changes you want done, let me know. We'll be here until about four putting on the finishing touches."

She couldn't imagine anything she would want changed, but while the two men talked business, she wandered around the drastically altered space. Admiring, touching, mentally filling the shelves and working behind the counters. She loved the sculpted molding and detail that precisely matched that of the bakery and marked it as hers.

Hers!

Well, hers and Aunt Helen's. And Marc's or the bank's, since she was sure there was going to be a hefty price to pay to someone at some point.

But even though she'd resisted being tied to her ex-husband in such a way, she couldn't deny that he had given her something no one else could—or would—have, and so quickly. She never would have been able to get things done in such short order with another investor or a loan directly from the bank.

Footsteps sounded behind her on the hardwood floor and she turned to see Marc coming toward her once again.

"They'll be cleaned up and out of here in a few more hours. And the computer equipment will be delivered tomorrow, so you can start setting up then, if you like."

Vanessa clasped her hands together, just barely resisting the urge to rub them together like some sort of devilish cartoon character. She was so excited, she almost couldn't contain herself.

They would need a website…and someone to design and maintain it, since she knew next to nothing about that sort of thing. They would also need packaging, and to set up an account with a reliable shipping company, and specialty shipping labels, and possibly even a catalog.

Goodness, there was so much to do. More, possibly, than she'd realistically considered.

Alarm began to claw at her insides and her chest became suddenly too tight to breathe. Oh, God, she couldn't do this. It was too much. She was only one person, for heaven's sake, and even if she counted on Aunt Helen's help, that made them only two people, one of whom had reached retirement age twenty years ago. Which basically put her back to being only one person, who *could not* handle this type of workload alone.

"I know you have a lot to do," Marc said, cutting into her panicked thoughts and allowing a small bit of oxygen to enter her lungs again, "but before you get too wrapped up in all of that, there's something I've been meaning to discuss with you."

She took a deep breath and forced herself to relax. One day at a time, one step at a time. She'd come this far, she could make it the rest of the way…even if it took her months to accomplish what a rich and powerful Keller heir could do practically overnight.

"All right."

"There's some company business that I need to return home to deal with."

"Oh." Her eyes widened in surprise.

She'd gotten so used to Marc being around that the idea of him leaving caught her unaware. Ironic, given how badly she'd wanted him to go back to Pittsburgh when he'd first arrived. Now, though, it was hard to picture the bakery or her day-to-day life without him in it.

Shaking off that rather revealing but unwelcome train of thought, she nodded her acceptance. "Okay, that's fine. I understand you have important work back in the city, and you've certainly done more than enough while you've been here."

She stopped herself just short of thanking him, but only because she was afraid that would fall too close to…well, thanking him, when he wasn't really doing her any favors. Oh, he'd been wonderfully helpful, but not out of the goodness of his heart. Better to take what he'd so generously offered and get him out of town before he started calling in vouchers and demanding repayment in ways she was unwilling or unable to fulfill.

A slow smile started to spread across his features and her pulse jumped. That wasn't a happy smile, it was an I-know-something-you-don't-know, cat-who-swallowed-the-canary smile.

"What?" she asked, drawing back slightly in wariness.

"You think I'm going to just pick up and leave, don't you?"

She had. Or perhaps she'd simply been hoping.

"It's all right, I understand," she said again. Sweeping an arm out to encompass their surroundings, she added, "This is all amazing, a wonderful start. Aunt Helen and I can certainly take over from here."

That smile stretched further, flashing bright white teeth, and a feeling of dread washed over her.

"I'm sure you and Aunt Helen will do a great job in getting the ball rolling. But that will have to wait until after we get back."

Vanessa blinked, replaying his words in her head. The feeling of dread started to dissipate, which was good...except that it seemed to be transforming into more of an all-over numbness that kept her brain from functioning properly.

She cleared her throat. "We?"

Marc inclined his head. "I want you and Danny to return to Pittsburgh with me so I can introduce my family to my son."

Eleven

"No."

Spinning on her heel, Vanessa stalked away, leaving Marc in the rippling wake of that cold, perfunctory response. Granted, he hadn't expected her to jump with joy at the prospect of going back with him, but he'd thought she would at least be reasonable about it.

With a sigh of resignation, he followed her through the plastic-draped doorway and into the bakery side of the building. She was already out of sight, likely in the kitchen, which meant she'd been moving at a pretty good clip.

He lifted a hand to push through the swinging door only to have it push back toward him, nearly cracking him in the face. Aunt Helen's blue eyes widened in startlement when she saw him, but she didn't say a word, simply tipped up her chin and pranced off for the front counter.

No love lost there, he thought, stepping into the kitchen and finding Vanessa exactly where he expected—standing at one of the large central islands, seemingly busy and focused on more food preparation. Even if she hadn't just walked away from him in a huff, he'd have known she was agitated by her jerky movements and the ramrod stiffness of her spine.

"Vanessa," he began, letting the door swing closed behind him.

"No."

She spat the word, then punctuated it with the slam of her rolling pin on the countertop. Cookie trays, cooling racks and miscellaneous utensils clattered against the stainless steel surface.

"No, Marc. No," she repeated with equal fervor, turning on him, her white-knuckled fingers still clinging to one of the rolling pin handles. "I am not going back there with you. I am not walking into that museum you call a home and dealing with your mother, who will look down her aristocratic nose at me just like she always has. And how much more judgmental and condescending do you think she'll be when you tell her I had a child out of wedlock? The fact that Danny is yours will be irrelevant. She'll criticize me for not telling you the minute I found out I was pregnant. She'll accuse me of going through with the divorce even though I knew I was carrying your baby, depriving you of time with your child and her of time with her grandchild. Of depriving *the world* of knowing about the existence of another great and wonderful Keller descendant."

Since that was pretty much exactly what he'd accused her of when *he'd* first learned of Danny's existence, he wasn't quite sure how to respond. Especially knowing how haughty his mother could be at times.

Vanessa let out a breath, seeming to lose a bit of her steam. In a lower, more subdued tone, she said, "Either that, or she'll deny Danny altogether. Declare he's not really a Keller, because of course she's always accused me of being a tramp, anyway. Or decide not to claim him as a Keller heir because we weren't married at the time of his birth."

She shook her head. "I won't do it, Marc. I won't go through that again and I sure as hell won't put my son through it."

Jaw clenching, he bit out, "He's my son, too, Vanessa."

"Yes," she acquiesced with a short nod of her head, "which is why you should want to protect him, too. From everything, and everyone."

Releasing the rolling pin, she put one hand flat to the island, the other on her hip and squared off, a mother bear ready and willing to protect her young, no matter what. "Danny is innocent. I won't let anyone make him feel less than perfect, less than wonderful. Ever. Not even his own grandmother."

Marc put his hands to his hips and cocked his head. "I had no idea you hated her so much," he murmured quietly.

"She was horrible to me," Vanessa retorted, rolling her eyes. "She made my life miserable while we were married."

For a minute, he didn't say anything, trying to gauge the truth of her words.

Had his mother really been that awful to her, or was Vanessa exaggerating? He knew women didn't always get along with their husbands' families and that mother-in-law/ daughter-in-law relationships could often be acrimonious.

Heaven knew his mother wasn't exactly the warmest person in the whole world, even with her own children, but had she really been so cruel to Vanessa when he hadn't been around?

"I'm sorry you feel that way," he said carefully, "but I have to go back. Not for long—a few days, maybe a week. And I'd like to take Danny with me."

At that, Vanessa opened her mouth and he knew another argument was coming.

"You can't really stop me from taking him along," he told

her flatly. "He's my son and you've kept him from me—and from my family—all this time. I think I deserve to take him home with me for a while."

Cocking his head, he fixed her with an intense, no-nonsense stare. "And we both know I don't need your permission."

"Are you threatening to take him from me?" she asked in a low voice.

"Do I need to?" he responded just as softly.

Though her mouth flattened in obvious anger, he could see the pulse beating frantically at her throat and her blue eyes glittering with emotion.

"It's just for a few days," he assured her again, feeling the odd need to wipe the fear and brimming tears from those eyes. "A week at the most. And you're more than welcome to come along, keep an eye on both of us. Why do you think I invited you in the first place?"

She licked her lips, swallowing hard. "You're going to make me do this, aren't you?" she asked in a wavering but resolved voice.

"I'm going to do this, with or without you. What part you play in the situation and how close an eye you keep on Danny is entirely up to you."

She gave him a look that clearly said she didn't think the choice he was giving her was any choice at all, but damned if he'd back down or go home, even for a short stay, without his son. He'd only just discovered he was a father; he wasn't going to walk away that easily.

Nor was he willing to let Danny out of his sight for that long. It might only be a handful of days by the calendar, but he'd gotten so used to seeing his son each and every day, to spending true quality time with him, that even twenty-four hours would feel like a lifetime at this point.

The same could be said of being away from Vanessa, he

supposed, but then, his attraction to her had never been in question.

No, his thoughts now had to be for his son. And though he would never intentionally cause his ex-wife this much anxiety or upset, he couldn't honestly be sure that she wouldn't pick up Danny and run with him the minute he drove out of town.

It would mean leaving her aunt and bakery and the life she'd built here in Summerville, but she'd kept Danny's existence from him once. What was to say she wouldn't try to *steal* the baby from him this time around?

There was also the small issue of her current physical condition. Like it or not, there *was* a chance she was pregnant again, and until he knew for sure one way or the other, he didn't intend to let her get away or keep another of his children a secret from him for a year or more.

Which meant that if he couldn't stay in Summerville and keep an eye on her and Danny every minute, then he would have to take Danny with him back to Pittsburgh. Vanessa could go along or not, but the one thing he could count on was that if Danny was with him, she wouldn't be hieing off to parts unknown.

Mouth set in a mulish slant, she mumbled, "This is extortion, you know."

He raised a brow and resisted the urge to chuckle. "I'd hardly call it that."

"What would you call it, then?"

"Fatherhood," he replied. "I'm simply exerting my parental rights. You remember what those are, don't you? They're what you denied me for the past year while you kept Danny to yourself."

He hadn't meant to let his bitterness over the past slip out, but he could tell by her expression that she'd heard it loud and clear.

"I'm not letting you take Danny anywhere without me," she said stubbornly.

Her implication being that if he insisted on taking Danny home to visit his family, she would be going along, however reluctantly.

"If you can be ready by tomorrow, we'll leave around noon."

"I'm not sure I can be ready quite that early."

Marc tipped his head and gave a short nod. "Fine, make it one o'clock, then."

The last thing Vanessa wanted to do was leave Summerville and the nice, tidy life she'd built for herself to return to the lion's den that was Keller Manor. It might have been only temporary—very temporary, if Marc's promise held true—but whether it was five days or only one, every minute was bound to feel like an eternity.

Which was why she didn't rush when it came to packing for herself and Danny. She took her time discussing her absence with Aunt Helen and setting up a couple of extra employees to cover for her, wanting to make sure The Sugar Shack really would run smoothly while she was away.

Then she actually solicited Marc's help in gathering everything they would need to take Danny on even a short trip. She was pretty sure he had no idea just how involved traveling with a baby could be.

While she decided about which of her own items and outfits to pack, she put him in charge of gathering up Danny's clothes and toys. Making sure they had enough diapers and wipes, bottles and formula. Blankets, booties, hats, infant sunscreen and more.

Vanessa kept thinking up new things to add to the list, hiding her amusement when Marc would begin to grumble and reminding him that returning to Pittsburgh was his idea.

They could skip all of the fuss and muss, if he'd only agree to let her—and Danny—stay in Summerville.

Each time the topic came up, however, any mention of canceling the trip or of his going without them simply caused his jaw to go taut, and he would silently return to collecting Danny's things or securing the safety seat in the back of his Mercedes.

By one the next day—because try as she might, she hadn't been able to postpone any longer—they were standing on the curb, ready to leave. Danny was in his car seat, kicking his legs and gumming his very own set of brightly colored plastic keys, while Marc waited near the front passenger door. A few feet farther along the sidewalk, Vanessa and Aunt Helen stood hand in hand.

"You're sure you want to do this?" her aunt asked in a hushed voice.

Oh, she was very sure she *didn't*. But she couldn't say that. Partly because she'd grudgingly agreed to go and partly because she didn't want Aunt Helen to worry about her.

"I'm sure," she lied, even though her fingers were chilled inside her aunt's solid grip. "It will be fine. Marc just wants to introduce Danny to his family and take care of some business with the company. We'll be back by the end of the week."

Aunt Helen raised a brow. "I hope so. Don't let them drag you down again, darling," she added softly. "You know what it did to you last time, living under that roof. Don't let it happen again."

A lump formed in Vanessa's throat, so large, she could barely swallow. Pulling her aunt close, she hugged her tightly and waited until she thought she could speak.

"I won't," she promised, blinking back tears.

When she could finally bring herself to pull away from her aunt's embrace, she turned toward Marc and the waiting car. Though she knew he was eager to get on the road, his expression gave away nothing of his inner thoughts or feelings.

"Ready to go?" he asked in an even tone.

Since her throat was still tight with emotion, she could only nod before climbing into the front seat. Once her legs were tucked safely inside, he closed the door for her and she reached for the safety belt while he moved around to the driver's side.

Flipping down the visor, she used the tiny rectangular mirror to make sure Danny was still okay, doing her best to ignore Marc's sudden, overpowering presence as he slipped behind the wheel.

How could she have forgotten how small cars were? Even given the roominess of his sleek, black Mercedes with its supple, tan leather interior, it suddenly felt as though all of the oxygen had been sucked out of the air, making it hard for her to draw a breath.

After fastening his own seat belt, Marc turned the key in the ignition and the engine purred to life. Rather than pull right out, though, as she'd expected, they simply sat there for a moment. So long, in fact, that she turned her head to look at him.

"Is something wrong?" she asked, thinking that perhaps they'd forgotten something. Although how that could even be possible, she didn't know. They'd packed just about everything *but* the kitchen sink, as the overstuffed trunk and half-stuffed backseat could attest.

"I know you don't want to do this," he said, his moss-green eyes glittering into hers. "But it's going to be all right."

She held his gaze for a moment, feeling that lump in her throat—which had finally started to recede—swell up again. Then she nodded before turning her attention back to the view straight in front of her.

But what she was really thinking was, *Famous last words.*

Because she didn't think there was any way that this little visit to Marc's family could possibly be anything less than a complete disaster.

Twelve

Unfortunately, the drive to Pittsburgh flew by much more quickly than Vanessa would have liked. Before she knew it, they were pulling up the long, oak-lined drive to Keller Manor.

Every inch of blacktop that passed beneath the Mercedes's tires made her heart beat faster and her stomach sink lower until she started to worry she might actually be sick.

Don't be sick, don't be sick, don't be sick, she told herself, taking deep, even breaths and praying the mantra would work.

Marc pulled to a stop beneath the wide porte cochere and within moments a young man was opening her door, offering a hand to help her out, then rushing to open the rear door so she could see to Danny. Marc had obviously called ahead to let the family know he—or perhaps they—would be coming.

She'd never seen this particular young man before, but then, Eleanor Keller tended to go through household staff faster than allergy sufferers went through facial tissues. Marc's mother also liked to have someone on hand to do her every bidding at the snap of her fingers. She employed gardeners, chefs, maids, a butler, an on-site mechanic and at least one personal assistant.

How many of them Vanessa would come in contact with during her stay was left to be seen, but one thing she did know was that she would treat them a heck of a lot better than Eleanor did. She would treat them like actual human beings rather than servants or robots programmed to be seen, but not heard, and to do exactly as they were told—nothing more and nothing less.

Coming around to her side of the Mercedes, Marc popped the trunk, then tossed his keys to the kid in the short red jacket that marked him as a Keller Manor employee. It even had a gold crest of sorts embroidered over the left breast pocket.

"We aren't traveling light," Marc told him, one corner of his mouth twisting upward. "But it all goes in my suite."

Vanessa opened her mouth to correct him. Marc had brought a single overnight case with him, while all the rest of the belongings filling the car were hers or Danny's. And they definitely did not belong in Marc's rooms.

But he apparently knew what she was about to say, because he pressed his index finger to her mouth, effectively cutting off her disagreement.

"They go in my rooms," he said again, so that only she could hear. "You and Danny will be staying there with me while we're here. No arguments."

Marc might be high-handed and controlling, but just because he said "no arguments" didn't mean she wasn't going to give him one. She opened her mouth again to do just that, but he covered her lips with a quick, hard kiss.

"No arguments," he repeated a shade more sternly. "It will be better for everyone involved. Trust me on this, okay?"

She so didn't want to. There was something deeply ingrained in her since their divorce that made her not want to trust him or listen to him or even believe a word he said.

But the fact was, she did trust him. Sharing a suite with him would be awkward and uncomfortable, but considering where this particular suite of rooms was located—inside the dreaded Keller mansion—it might actually be safer than staying in a room of her own. In addition to being quite spacious, Marc's suite also happened to be the one they'd lived in together while they were married, so at least she would be in a familiar setting.

"Fine," she muttered, slightly distracted by the lingering remnants of his kiss. He tasted of mint, and she could have sworn it was of the mentholated variety, because her lips were still tingling from the contact, however brief.

"Good," he replied, looking much too pleased with himself for her peace of mind. Then he scooped Danny out of her arms, tucking him against his own chest. "Now let's go inside and introduce our son to the rest of his family."

At that, Vanessa's stomach started to pitch and roll again, but Marc reached for her hand and the warmth of his fingers clasping hers was as calming as a glass of merlot. Well, almost. She was still jittery and her breathing was shallow as they stepped through the wide, white double front doors.

Built of redbrick and tall, Grecian columns, the entire mansion looked like a throwback to *Gone with the Wind*'s Tara—pre-Civil War destruction, of course. Secretly, however, Vanessa had always thought Marc's mother was trying to compete with a much larger residence, like the White House. And was winning.

Just inside the main entrance, the foyer sparkled like the lobby of a grand hotel. The parquet floor had been waxed to a high gloss. The chandelier hanging overhead glittered with polish and a thousand bits of glass shaped like teardrops reflecting the light of another thousand brightly lit bulbs.

In the center of the floor, an enormous display of freshly cut flowers rested on a sizeable marble table. And behind that, a wide, curved staircase was only one of the many ways to get to the second floor and opposite wings of the house.

It all looked exactly as it had the day Vanessa had left. Even the bouquet, which was large enough to bring Seabiscuit to his knees, was the same. Oh, they were different flowers, she was sure; Eleanor had new ones delivered every morning for the entire house. But they were the same *type* of flowers, the same colors, the very same arrangement.

She'd been gone a year. A year in which just about everything in her life had changed substantially. But if not even the flowers in the Keller's foyer had changed, she had little hope that anything—or anyone—else under the mansion's million-dollar roof had.

They didn't have coats, so the butler who had opened the door for them moved on down the long hallway to one side of the stairwell—likely to alert his mistress to their arrival. Seconds later, he returned to help the young man who was unloading the car carry their things to Marc's suite.

A moment after they disappeared upstairs, Eleanor emerged from her favorite parlor.

"Marcus, darling," she greeted Marc—and only Marc.

At the sound of her ex-mother-in-law's voice, Vanessa's heart lurched and she murmured a quick prayer asking for the strength and patience to get through this agonizing visit with the Wicked Witch of Western Pennsylvania.

The witch in question was dressed in a beige skirt and jacket over a pristine white blouse, all of which likely cost more than The Sugar Shack's monthly profits. Her hair was a perfect brownish-blond bob and her diamond jewelry— earrings, necklace, lapel pin and one ring—all matched and were no doubt very, very real. Eleanor Keller would never stoop to wearing cubic zirconia or costume jewelry, not even on an ordinary, uneventful weekday.

"Mother," Marc returned, leaning in to peck each of the older woman's cheeks. Bouncing Danny slightly in his arms, he added, "Meet your newest grandchild, Daniel Marcus."

Eleanor's pinched mouth twisted into what Vanessa suspected was meant to be a smile. "Lovely," she intoned, not even bothering to reach out and touch the baby. She simply perused him from head to toe.

Vanessa stiffened, offended on her child's behalf. But then Eleanor's attention shifted to her and she knew she would soon be offended on her very own behalf.

"I don't know what you were thinking," Marc's mother chastised, "keeping my son's child from him all this time. You should have said something the moment you discovered you were pregnant. You had no right to keep a Keller heir to yourself."

And it begins, Vanessa thought, with no sense of surprise whatsoever. She also wasn't offended, though she knew she had every right. Probably because Eleanor's reaction to her reappearance was exactly what she'd expected.

"Mother," Marc snapped in a tone Vanessa had rarely, if ever, heard from him.

Vanessa turned her head to study him, stunned by the look of anger on his face.

"We discussed this when I called," he continued. "The circumstances surrounding Danny's birth are between Vanessa and myself. I won't have you insulting her while we're here. Is that understood?"

Vanessa watched with wide eyes while Eleanor's lips flattened into a thin, unhappy line.

"Very well," she replied. "Dinner will be served at six

o'clock. I'll leave you both to get settled. And please remember that we *dress* for meals in this house."

After flicking a disdainful glance over Vanessa's modest outfit of magenta slacks and sleeveless polka-dot blouse, Marc's mother turned on her heel and clicked her way back across the parquet floor.

Releasing a pent-up breath, Vanessa muttered, "That went well."

She meant it to be sarcastic, but Marc simply smiled.

"I told you so." Hiking a drowsy Danny higher on his shoulder, he said, "Let's go upstairs and unpack. I think Danny could use a bit of a nap, too."

Reaching out, she brushed a hand over her son's brown, baby-soft hair. "He shouldn't be tired, he slept in the car."

Marc flashed her a grin. "It didn't take."

She chuckled, because she couldn't seem to help herself. This was the Marc she remembered from when they'd first started dating, first been married. Funny, kind, thoughtful... and so handsome, he took her breath away.

Warmth suffused her as he took her hand and started toward the wide stairwell. It spread from her fingertips to every other part of her body, making her tingle, and bringing up all sorts of wonderful memories.

How could being this close to Marc again feel so good, so right, when being in this house again felt so very wrong?

Marc watched Vanessa move around his suite, getting ready for dinner. Danny was sleeping in the sitting room, in a crib that had been set up at his request before their arrival.

But it was his ex-wife's presence that had his gut clenching and his mind spinning. She looked right here. It *felt* right to have her here again.

He wasn't sure he meant *here* as in his family's home,

though. It wasn't about having her back at the Keller Manor, or even in his private suite under his family's roof.

It was about having her with him, in his bedroom, no matter where that room happened to be located.

He'd missed that. Missed seeing her things spread out on top of the bureau and cluttering the bathroom vanity. Having her clothes hanging with his in the closet, the scent of her perfume lightly permeating his work shirts and the sheets on the bed.

He'd missed simply watching her, like this, as she moved around the room getting dressed, fixing her hair, doing her makeup or choosing which pieces of jewelry to wear.

Granted, she didn't have as many of those things with her this time as she had when they'd been man and wife, but that didn't keep her from falling into the same old habits or her movements from being achingly familiar. She was even wearing her favorite perfume—probably because she'd left a bottle on the dresser when she'd moved out and he hadn't been able to bring himself to get rid of it.

Now, he was glad. He'd given it to her for their anniversary, after all. So very long ago, it seemed. But the fact that she was wearing it again, that she was here with him, and apparently still trusted him… It made him wonder if maybe they could work out their differences and give each other another chance.

"How do I look?" she asked suddenly, breaking into his thoughts.

"Beautiful," he replied, without having to think about it, without even having to look. Though he did—long and hard. Looking at her was always a pleasure.

She was wearing a simple yellow sundress and sandals, with her hair pulled back above her ears so that her natural copper curls were even more prominent. His blood stirred in his veins, arousal pouring through him, and he licked his lips, wishing he could lick *her*—like a sweet, lemon-flavored popsicle.

Her eyes turned smoky and she offered him a small, sultry smile before brushing her hands down the sides of her skirt.

"Are you sure? You know what your mother is like and I didn't really pack anything dressy. I should have remembered her rule about formal dinners."

She paused to take a breath, then blew it out and wiped her hands on her skirt again in that same nervous gesture. "Of course, I don't have very many formal clothes anymore, so I couldn't have packed them even if I'd wanted to. I thought maybe some of my old clothes would still be here, but…"

She trailed off, her gaze skittering away from his, and Marc felt a stab of guilt somewhere around his solar plexus.

"I'm sorry. Mother had them thrown out after you left. I didn't expect you to be back, so I didn't think to keep any of them."

The truth was, they'd been too painful a reminder of her. Of her desertion, of the divorce papers he'd signed willingly more out of anger than any real desire to be single again and of the happier times they'd had together before things had somehow gone terribly wrong.

He shouldn't have let his mother dispose of them, he realized that now. It had been his place to deal with them, and he probably should have tracked Vanessa down to see if she wanted any of the items shipped to her before having them carted away. But at the time, he'd just wanted them gone and had been almost relieved when his mother had declared it was time to rid the house of any reminders of his ex-wife's abandonment.

The only thing that had been left behind was that crystal decanter of perfume.

"You look beautiful," he repeated, striding across the thickly carpeted floor to grasp her shoulders. "And we're not here to impress anyone. Not even Mother," he added with a grin.

When her mouth twitched with the beginnings of a smile and at least some of the anxiety seemed to drain away from her features, he leaned in and kissed her. He kept it light, even though that was far from what he really wanted.

Just the firm press of lips to lips instead of a ravaging of tongues. Just the brush of his fingertips over the warm skin of her bare shoulders instead of his hands delving inside her bodice and beneath the hem of her skirt.

He lingered for a few precious, breathless moments, then released her, stepping back before the full proof of his desire for her became obvious. Her freshly applied lipstick was smudged and he reached out to brush a spot with the edge of his thumb.

"Maybe we should skip dinner and go straight to dessert," he suggested in a low, graveled voice.

"I don't think your mother would like that very much."

He was pleased to hear the same huskiness in her voice as in his own. It meant he wasn't alone in the passion causing his pulse to hammer and hum.

"I don't think I give a good damn," he muttered with no small amount of feeling behind the words.

"As bad an idea as that probably is, I sincerely wish we could. Anything would be better than having to face your mother again."

The corner of Marc's mouth quirked down in a frown. Was she implying that staying in the room to make love with him would be only slightly less miserable than an evening spent in his family's company? He wasn't sure he liked being considered the lesser of two evils.

Before he had a chance to reply, however, a tapping sounded on the suite's outer door.

"That will be the nanny," he said, just managing to mask a sigh of disappointment.

"You hired a nanny?" Vanessa asked, sounding both surprised and disapproving.

"Not really," he replied. "One of Mother's maids is going to sit with him for a couple of hours. That's all right, isn't it?"

Her brows crossed. "I don't know. Is she good with infants?"

"I don't know," he said, repeating her phrase. "Let's go meet her and give her the third degree."

Wrapping his hand around her elbow, he pulled her with him toward the bedroom door.

"I don't want to give her the third degree," Vanessa murmured softly as they crossed the sitting room where Danny was sleeping. "I just want to know that she's qualified to sit with my child."

"We'll be right downstairs, so you can come up and check on her any time you like," he assured her, keeping his voice equally low. "Tonight can be her test run. If you like her and she does a good job, she can stay with Danny whenever you need her while you're here. If not, we'll hire a real nanny. One you feel a hundred percent confident in."

"You're placating me, aren't you?" she asked, an edge of annoyance entering her tone.

With his hand on the knob of the sitting room door, he turned to her and smiled. "Absolutely. While you're here, whatever you need, whatever you want, I intend to see that you get it."

Her eyes widened and he knew she was about to argue. So he bent down and captured her mouth, kissing her into warm and pliant submission.

When he pulled away, his own body was buzzing with warmth, but he was far from pliant. Quite stiff and unyielding would have been more accurate.

"Indulge me," he said, brushing a stray copper curl behind her ear while the taste of her lingered on his lips and prodded him to kiss her again. "Please."

Thirteen

As always, dinner with Marc's family was exhausting. Delicious, but exhausting.

Marc's mother was her usual haughty self, and though Vanessa had always liked Marc's brother Adam and Adam's wife, Clarissa, they were cut from the same basic cloth as Eleanor. Born with silver spoons in their mouths, they'd never known a moment of true want or need. And being raised as they had been, they were extremely refined, never a hair out of place, never a wrong word spoken.

The only reason Vanessa felt kindly toward them at all was that, despite their upbringings, Adam and Clarissa weren't quite as cold and judgmental as her ex-mother-in-law. From the moment she'd married Marc, they'd treated her like a true member of the family and had seemed genuinely sorry when she and Marc had split up.

Even tonight, knowing the circumstances surrounding Vanessa's return to Keller Manor and Eleanor's obvious disdain for her, Marc's brother and sister-in-law had treated her exactly the same as they had in the past. No sidelong glances or sharply pointed questions meant to put her on the spot or make her feel insecure, just friendly smiles and harmless banter.

That alone had helped to assuage some of Vanessa's raw and rampaging nerves when she'd first walked into the opulent dining room. Of course, Eleanor had already been seated at the head of the table like a queen holding court—and her expression alone had made Vanessa feel like a bug under a microscope.

To Vanessa's relief, her former mother-in-law had played fair through the soup and salad courses, keeping conversation light and impersonal. There were a couple of sticky moments while they enjoyed their entrees, but by the time dessert was being served, Eleanor dropped her semi-polite facade and began taking potshots at Vanessa as often as she thought she could get away with it. Some of them were direct, others more passive-aggressively delivered.

But this time, Marc actually stuck up for her—something he'd never done before, not with his mother. Possibly because in the past, Eleanor's attacks had been much more subtle, and often reserved for moments when the two of them were alone so that no one else would witness her true hatred for her son's wife.

Marc had grown up under Eleanor's frosty disposition, so he was used to her testy personality and jagged barbs. Even though her mother-in-law's malicious treatment had cut her to the quick, Vanessa truly believed that much of what Marc witnessed had gone straight over his head. He was like someone raised in the city, who wouldn't be bothered by the sounds of round-the-clock street traffic the way someone would who'd been raised in the quietness of the country.

But tonight, Marc hadn't let his mother's not-so-subtle

assaults slide by. He'd caught and responded to every one, always in Vanessa's defense. And once dessert was finished, when Eleanor seemed to be working herself toward a full-blown attack, he'd announced that it had been a long day, wished his family good-night, and taken Vanessa's hand to lead her out of the dining room.

She was almost giddy with relief and unaccustomed empowerment…and was still clutching his hand like a life preserver as they jogged upstairs side by side. She felt like she had when they'd first been dating, before the realities of being Mrs. Marcus Keller had settled around her and robbed her of her happiness.

Reaching the door to his suite, they were both smiling, and she was slightly out of breath. He put a finger to his lips, signaling for her to be quiet before he opened the door.

The fact that he had to remind her to be silent made her realize how close to giggling she was. *Giggling.* Like a twelve-year-old.

Biting back the strangled sound, she kept hold of Marc's hand and followed him into the darkened sitting room. The maid-slash-nanny they'd left with Danny was sitting across the room from the crib, reading a magazine beneath the muted yellow glare of a single low-lit lamp. When she saw them, she closed the magazine and quickly rose to her feet.

"How was he?" Marc whispered.

"Just fine," the young woman answered with a small smile. "He slept the entire time."

Good news for a babysitter. Not such good news for parents who were looking forward to a full night's sleep.

"That means he'll be up in the middle of the night," Vanessa whispered to no one in particular. And then to Marc, she said, "Prepare yourself for finally experiencing the true rigors of fatherhood."

He flashed her a grin, his green eyes sparking with a blaze

of heat that had nothing to do with parental exhilaration. "I'm looking forward to it."

After slipping the young maid a couple of folded-up bills that Vanessa was sure Eleanor would disapprove of, he saw her out, then joined Vanessa at the side of Danny's crib. His hand came up to rest on the small of her back, and she had to swallow a lump of emotion at the picture they must have made. Mother and father standing at the edge of their infant son's crib, watching him sleep.

This was what she'd always imagined motherhood and family would be like. It's what she'd wanted when she'd married Marc and they'd first started trying to get pregnant.

Funny how life never quite turned out the way you planned.

But this was nice, too. Maybe not ideal, maybe not the epitome of her adolescent dreams, but it still warmed her and made her heart swell inside her chest.

"I hope he's not coming down with something," she murmured, putting the back of her hand to Danny's tiny forehead. He didn't feel feverish, but one could never tell. "He doesn't usually sleep this long."

"He's had a busy day," Marc offered just as softly. "You'd be tired, too, if this were your first big trip since being born."

She chuckled, then had to cover her mouth to keep from waking the baby. With a grin of his own, Marc grabbed her arm and tugged her toward the bedroom door.

Once they were safely inside, he twirled her around and pushed her up against the hard, flat panel, covering her mouth with his own. His arms on either side of her head boxed her in, his body pressing her flat and sending a flare of heat everywhere he touched.

For long minutes, he kissed her, their breaths mingling, his tongue thrusting, parrying, drawing her into his passionate duel. She lost her breath, her vision, her sanity, her entire world shrinking to the single pinprick of reality that was Marc's solid embrace.

When he lightened his hold enough to let her gasp for air, she blinked like a newborn foal and let her head fall back against the door while he continued to nibble at her loose, tingling lips.

"This isn't what I had in mind when you said we'd be sharing your rooms," she managed—barely—after filling her lungs with a gasp of much-needed oxygen.

"Funny. It's exactly what I pictured." He murmured the words against her skin, moving to suckle the lobe of her ear around her small hoop earring.

Somehow she didn't doubt that. But letting his mother think they were sharing a room and *actually* sharing a room—a bed—were two completely different things.

"I was going to sleep on the chaise in the other room. Or slip into one of the guest rooms when nobody was looking. This…"

She moaned as his tongue darted out to lick a line of electricity from her collarbone to the hollow behind her ear. The sensation shot through her like a shock wave, turning her knees to jelly.

"Not smart. Not smart at all," she wheezed, unsure of whether the words were actually coming out of her mouth or simply echoing through her rapidly liquefying brain.

Shifting to wrap his arms around her and lift her against his body—one hand at her back, the other cradling her bottom—he turned and strode directly to the bed.

"I think it's positively brilliant," he replied, and then dropped her to the mattress like a sack of potatoes.

She certainly didn't *feel* like a sack of potatoes, though. Not when he followed her down, covering her from chest to ankle with his hot, heavy bulk.

This time, when he kissed her, she didn't think to protest where all of this might be leading. Maybe because she *knew* where it was leading. They both did.

Or maybe because his mouth on hers, his hands on her body, drove every other rational thought straight out of her head.

With deft fingers, he untied the knot of her dress's bodice behind her neck, lowering the gauzy yellow material to reveal her braless breasts. He cupped them together, kneading, brushing the tight nipples with his thumbs until she moaned and wiggled beneath him.

He returned her moan with one of his own, then let his hands slide around her waist to the rear zipper. She rose slightly and waited for the gentle *snick-snick-snick-snick* to stop, for him to tug the full skirt past her hips and thighs. Lifting himself up, he pulled the dress completely off, then divested her of her strappy sandals, as well.

She lay there in only a pair of thin, silken panties. They weren't the sexiest thing she'd ever worn, but she thanked heaven she was past the "granny panty" phase of pregnancy and new motherhood.

Judging by Marc's expression, he approved. For long minutes, he stayed propped on one strong arm staring down at her with eyes that had gone dark and primal. A shiver stole over her at that look, at the way it made her feel.

Not helpless or vulnerable by any means. Instead, she felt powerful. That she could incite that level of heat and lust in him continued to amaze her.

It had been that way in the beginning, and for most of their marriage, but she wouldn't have expected such intense desire to still be there after all they'd been through. That it was felt a bit like a miracle, even though she had no idea how the passion they shared in the bedroom could possibly translate to their future everyday lives.

His fingers delving beneath the elastic waist of her underwear dragged her up from the quagmire of her inner thoughts, and she was more than willing to grab hold of the life rope he offered.

She let him snake the panties down her legs, laying her bare, and then wrapped her arms around his neck to pull him down for a deep, soulful kiss. With a groan, Marc ground the bulge of his still-trapped erection against her hip.

Shifting beneath him, she welcomed him into the cradle of her thighs, crossing her legs behind his waist. He groaned again—or maybe it was a growl—and pressed even closer.

There was something between them, Marc thought. Something compelling and meaningful and not to be taken for granted. And he realized suddenly that that's exactly what he'd done—he'd taken his relationship with Vanessa for granted.

He'd married her, and brought her home, and simply assumed she would always be there. How could she not be happy in a house roughly the size of Buckingham Palace on an estate that boasted a tennis court, movie theater, two swimming pools—one indoors, one out—a riding stable, gardens, walking paths, a pond…everything anyone could ever want. Add to that the fact that he had more money than Midas and Croesus combined and he'd thought there was nothing he couldn't offer her, no reason any woman would ever walk away from him.

He'd never been one to delve too deeply into his or anyone else's feelings, but these past few weeks had him thinking differently. Feeling things he'd never felt before and wondering things he'd never thought to wonder about.

Maybe money wasn't everything. Maybe situating Vanessa in his family's mansion and giving her *carte blanche* with his primary bank account hadn't been enough for her.

But wasn't that a good thing? Didn't it mean that she hadn't loved him for his money alone? For what he had or what he could give her?

He wasn't sure what to think of that, since he was rich and intended to stay that way.

What he did know was that some sort of bond obviously still existed between them.

It wasn't just the sex—although that alone was outstanding enough to give him pause. But whatever it was, still buzzing and humming whenever they were together, it warranted a few hours of serious consideration.

Was there a chance they could reconcile? Try again, start over, build something better and stronger than they'd had before?

But even if they could, should they?

It was too much to contemplate rationally at the moment, given that his mind was currently preoccupied with more immediate and infinitely more enjoyable pursuits. But he did need to think about it. Decide if what he thought he was feeling was real.

Because what he thought he was feeling was love. Love. Longing. Devotion. And a desire to once again make things with Vanessa permanent.

He groaned as her tongue swirled inside his mouth and her ankles tightened at the small of his back. The heat of her naked body burned through his clothes and suddenly he wanted them gone.

With her still clinging to him like plastic wrap, he reached between them to tug at the buttons of his shirt, his belt, the front of his slacks. She shifted when necessary, giving him the space to shrug out of his clothes with jerky movements, but never actually letting go.

Once he was as naked as she, he edged her higher on the bed, careful not to bump her into the headboard while he held her to him with one arm and rearranged the overstuffed pillows with the other. He propped a couple under her rear, lifting her so that she looked down on him and the short strands of her copper hair fell around his face, as well as her own.

Grasping her chin, he held her in place while he nibbled her lips, tracing patterns over her waist and back with his fingertips. Her skin was like the smooth perfection of an alabaster statue, all elegant dips and curves. Only where statues were cold and lifeless, Vanessa was anything but. She was passionate and beautiful, and the only woman he'd ever made love to here, in this bed.

Before their marriage, he hadn't bothered to bring women home with him, at least not in order to sleep with them. It had been easier and less complicated to limit any intimacies to their apartments or the occasional hotel room. Even with those he'd dated seriously.

After the divorce…well, the truth was that he hadn't been with another woman since Vanessa left. He'd thrown himself into his work and the company. Frankly, no one else had even remotely caught his interest in the past year. He wondered now if anyone else ever would.

Crossing his arms behind her back, he grasped her to him, flattening her full, round breasts to his chest. She ran her hands through his hair, raking her nails over his scalp and the nape of his neck, something he'd always loved. It sent shivers of arousal down his spine and blood pulsing even more heavily between his legs.

Feeling the twitch of his erection, Vanessa shifted on his lap, arranging herself at a better angle to hover just above him. She wrapped her slim fingers around his hard length and stroked him lightly for a moment before guiding him ever so slowly into her damp, welcoming warmth.

Marc hissed a breath through clenched teeth, reciting stock values in his head to keep the evening from being over much too soon. The feel of her surrounding him, of being buried inside her, was one of the most astonishing sensations he'd ever experienced. No matter how many times it happened, each was nearly a religious experience. Amazing and life-altering. Impossibly better than the time before, and certain never to be as mind-blowing again.

She fit him like a glove, snug and hot, clutching at him in a way that nearly sent the top of his head spinning off. Hands on her bare buttocks, he tugged her closer—not that there was more than the thinnest sliver of space between them to begin with. But if he could have absorbed her into him, he would have.

Her breath whooshed out as she hit his chest with a *thump*, but he didn't give her a chance to refill her lungs with fresh air. Instead, he took her mouth while he lifted her up…and down. Up…and down. Short, jerky movements at first that grew faster and more frantic as their passions built and their mingled breathing became ragged.

Marc's heart pounded beneath his rib cage, every cell in his body tightening, straining, striving for release. He fought it, wanting the feelings to last. Wanting this time with Vanessa to last.

But holding back his orgasm was like trying to hold back a monsoon. His only hope was to hang on long enough and make sure she was with him when it happened.

Reaching between them, he trailed the flat of his hand over her abdomen and slipped two fingers into her folds in search of the secret bundle of nerves that would send her over the edge. She gasped as soon as he touched her there and he felt her inner muscles clench around him.

He cursed under his breath, working to school his breathing and praying for just a little more staying power. Just a little more.

Using the pads of those two fingers, he circled the swollen

bud first one direction and then the other. Vanessa gave a long, plaintive moan, her spine bowing as she arched above him.

"That's it, baby," he panted, cocking his hips to meet her every downward thrust. "Let yourself go. Come with me."

Her body was growing taut, her movements and breathing becoming more and more frenetic as her climax approached. Marc continued to tease, continued to drive her higher and higher. Pinching, flicking, letting his nails rake across her most sensitive spot while he rocked her from below.

And then she was over, crying out as wave after wave of pleasure rippled through her, causing her to shudder from head to toe.

Marc wasn't far behind. As soon as he felt the start of her climax, he released the stranglehold on his own self-control, and followed her into bliss.

Fourteen

Vanessa awoke to early morning sunlight streaming through the half-drawn draperies and across the bed. A wide smile split her face as she stretched like a cat, feeling better than she had in a very long time.

Tilting her head, she checked the clock, then sat up quickly. Ten o'clock! How could she possibly have slept so long?

Granted, she'd had a rather rigorous evening. She and Marc had made love three times during the long night, and Danny had had them both out of bed a couple of times in between. But she still should have been up long before now, especially since Danny *had* to be awake and fussing.

Rolling to the edge of the mattress, she started to sit up only to have her hand bump something near the head of the bed. It crinkled slightly, and when she looked, she found a slip of paper lying half under Marc's pillow.

Had to go to the office, it said in her ex-husband's tall, distinctive scrawl. *Danny is with Marguerite. Home for dinner.* And it was signed, *Love, M.*

Short and to the point, which was typical of Marc. But using the L-word in a frivolous manner was not. Did he mean it? Or had it simply slipped out by habit, given their return to familiar marital intimacies?

Vanessa's heart pinched inside her chest. She wasn't sure how to feel about either possibility, so she decided not to think about it too much. At least not at the moment.

Slipping out of bed, she quickly dressed in a pair of linen slacks and a light pumpkin orange top, then made her way out of the suite and downstairs, peeking her head in several doorways as she went in hopes of finding Danny.

She found them in the library. A large blanket was spread out on the floor with Danny in the center. Toys were spread all around, and the same young maid from last evening sat at one corner, making faces and playing with the laughing child. She was definitely working overtime, Vanessa thought, making a mental note to ask Marc if she was being properly compensated.

"Ms. Keller," the woman murmured as soon as she spotted Vanessa. Pushing to her feet, she clasped her hands nervously behind her back.

"It's Mason, actually," Vanessa replied automatically. Moving toward the blanket, she knelt beside Danny and scooped him up, cradling him against her chest.

He giggled, kicked his little legs and grabbed for her hair. She chuckled in return, kissing one of his warm, chubby cheeks.

"Thank you for watching him again," she said, climbing back to her feet and taking a seat on one of the nearby sofas.

"My pleasure, ma'am. Mr. Keller said it was all right to

give him a bottle and some baby cereal, so he's been fed and burped. Changed, too."

Vanessa nodded, sending the young woman a gentle smile. Her first inclination was to dismiss the maid and take over Danny's care herself. She wasn't used to having staff on hand and underfoot anymore to see to her every need or whim. And she *was* used to taking care of things—especially her son— almost single-handedly.

But the maid looked so eager to please and Vanessa knew from personal experience how demanding Eleanor could be. She was hard enough on her children and their spouses, but with her employees, she was downright tyrannical.

Standing, she gave Danny another kiss, this one in the center of his forehead, then returned him to the blanket.

"Would you mind watching him for a while longer?" she asked as she straightened. "I'd like to get some breakfast."

The young maid looked both pleased and unaccountably relieved. She quickly moved back to the blanket and took up her post at Danny's side.

"Of course, ma'am. Take your time."

"Thank you."

As familiar as Vanessa was with Keller Manor, she was anything but comfortable inside its gates and walls. It was too big and lifeless for her tastes, reminding her of some cold, cavernous mausoleum. At times, she could swear her footsteps and voice actually echoed as if she was inside a giant catacomb.

Although she knew she could go straight to the dining room, and a servant would be there to take her order in under a minute, she instead made her way to the kitchen at the rear of the house. The kitchen staff was busy bustling around, cleaning up from the rest of the family's morning meal and preparing for the afternoon one.

"Ms. Keller," one of them chirped when she saw her.

Vanessa smiled, not bothering to correct the use of her married name. If she did that every time one of the staff reverted to the family surname, she would get nothing else done.

"Hello, Glenna. It's nice to see you again."

The older woman's smile was warm and genuine, not the usual lift of dutiful lips. "You, too, ma'am."

"How many times have I told you to call me Vanessa?" she scolded with a friendly wink.

The woman nodded, but old habits died hard, and Vanessa knew every one of the Keller staff would rather be chastised by her for *not* calling her by her first name than to accidentally slip and call Eleanor by hers.

"I missed breakfast. Do you think I could get a slice of toast and some juice?" she asked. She knew better than to try to fix something on her own. She'd done that before, when she and Marc had first been married, and learned very quickly that the kitchen staff could be more than a little territorial.

"Of course, ma'am."

Glenna bustled off to fix a tray while Vanessa climbed onto a stool right there at the center island. She could have gone off to the dining room to wait, but the room was so large and empty, whereas the kitchen felt homier and buzzed with energy. She could also do without bumping into Eleanor, which was more likely elsewhere in the house.

After taking her time with *two* slices of toast and a scrambled egg because Glenna insisted she could use the protein, Vanessa strolled back to the library. Marguerite was still there, and Danny was still playing and cooing, enjoying himself just as much as when she'd left.

She laughed herself, just looking at him. There were few things in the world as delightful as a baby's heartfelt giggle, and she never grew tired of hearing her own child expressing his happiness over some silly thing like a shaken rattle or a game of peekaboo.

Joining them on the blanket, she spent the next twenty or thirty minutes entertaining Danny and chatting with Marguerite, who turned out to be a college student trying to earn extra money for tuition over her summer break. Vanessa could certainly relate, since that's exactly what she'd been doing when she'd met Marc for the first time.

"Well, isn't this a sweet little tableau."

Eleanor's crisp tone and deceptively reproving words cut Marguerite off midsentence and sent a flush of guilt toward the young maid's hairline. She immediately jumped up, fidgeting nervously.

"You may go," Eleanor told her without preamble.

Marguerite gave a quick nod, mumbled, "Yes, ma'am," and hurried out of the room.

Vanessa was just as uncomfortable with her ex-mother-in-law's sudden appearance, but refused to let it show. She certainly wasn't going to rush to her feet like some loyal subject in front of her reigning queen.

Remaining where she was, she continued playing with Danny, fighting the morbid impulse to glance in the older woman's direction.

"You didn't have to scare her off, Eleanor," she said flatly, finally looking up at her. "She's a nice girl. We were having an interesting conversation."

If possible, Eleanor's features turned even more pinched and disapproving. "I've told you before that it's unseemly to make friends with the help."

Vanessa chuckled at that, a short burst of unexpected sound that caused the older woman's brows to pucker. "I'm afraid I don't adhere to your antiquated rules, especially since I used to *be* the help, remember?"

"Oh, I remember," Eleanor replied coolly.

Of course, she did. Wasn't that her number one complaint about Vanessa ending up married to her son? That a high and mighty Keller heir might stoop so low as to tie himself to a common, no-name waitress?

"Do you really think this is going to work out?" Eleanor continued snidely. "That you can hide my son's child from him for nearly a year, then simply bat your eyes and waltz back into the lap of luxury, trapping Marcus all over again?"

Keeping one hand on Danny's belly and rubbing him gently through the soft cotton of his teddy bear onesie tucked into a tiny pair of denim shorts, Vanessa finally turned her head to meet her ex-mother-in-law's stern, steel-gray gaze. "Contrary to your single-minded beliefs, I don't particularly consider Keller Manor the lap of luxury. You may have everything money can buy, but this house definitely isn't a home. There's no warmth here and very little love."

She paused for a moment to lift Danny against her chest before climbing to her feet. Turning, she faced Eleanor head-on. "And I'm not trying to *trap* Marc. I never was. I just wanted to love him and be happy. But you couldn't let that happen, could you?"

Shifting Danny higher on her hip, she hugged him close and continued with so much of what she'd been wanting to say for years. "God forbid Marc falls in love with a woman from the wrong side of the tracks, with red blood instead of blue running through her veins. God forbid he be happy and make his own decisions and get out from under your oppressive, all-powerful thumb."

The words poured out of her like a rainstorm, but even though a sliver of fear remained at the very pit of her belly, she also felt relieved…and stronger than she would have expected.

Why hadn't she found the courage to tell Eleanor off long before now? She might have saved her marriage. Saved herself countless tears. Saved them all months and months of misery.

Eleanor, of course, didn't take Vanessa's first act of independence at all well. Her cheeks turned an unseemly shade of pink while her eyes narrowed and her jaw locked like a piranha's.

"How dare you?" she seethed, her face turning even more mottled.

But her anger didn't faze Vanessa. Not anymore.

"I should have dared a long time ago. I should have stood up to you and refused to let you intimidate me just because you come from old money and are used to looking down your nose at people. And I should have told Marc how you were treating me from the very beginning instead of trying to keep the peace and avoid tarnishing his opinion of you."

She shook her head, sad but determined. "I was young and stupid then, but I've grown up a lot in the past year. And I have a child of my own now...one I don't intend to let you push around, or let witness you pushing *me* around. I'm sorry, Eleanor, but if you want to be in your grandson's life, you're going to have to start treating me with a little respect."

Vanessa could tell from the pinch of her ex-mother-in-law's lips that she was about as far from that happening as from flapping her arms and flying to the moon.

"Get. Out."

Eleanor spat the words like a fire-breathing dragon, as though they were two completely different sentences. Fury shook her from head to toe, and if she'd had any medical issues, Vanessa would have worried she was on the verge of suffering a heart attack or stroke.

"Get out of my house," she repeated, turning to point one long, diamond-adorned finger toward the door.

Not that Vanessa had to be told twice.

"Gladly," she said, bending at the waist to gather Danny's blanket and toys one-handedly.

With her shoulders back and her head held high, she strode past Eleanor and up the long stairwell to Marc's suite to pack her things.

Marc pulled his Mercedes in front of the house and cut the engine. Normally he would drive around to the garage, but he was only going to be a few minutes. He'd forgotten some files on the desk in his suite, and was hoping he had time to grab them, get back to the office, deal with the rest of the issues filling his long to-do list and get home again in time for dinner.

Normally, he would simply skip dinner with the family and remain at the office as long as it took to get the job done. But for some reason, his workaholic temperament seemed to have abandoned him. He barely wanted to spend the rest of the day at the office, let alone his evening, as well. Instead, he wanted to be here, at home, with Vanessa and Danny.

His mouth curved in a smile just thinking about them, and he glanced at his watch, debating how much time he could afford to spend with them before turning around and heading back into the city.

There was a taxi parked ahead of him in the driveway and he lifted a hand to the cabbie as he rounded his Mercedes, wondering what it was doing there. Perhaps his mother had visitors, though it was odd for any of her acquaintances not to have their own very expensive, chauffeured vehicles.

Bounding up the front steps, he pushed open the door and came to a screeching halt at the pile of luggage and baby items in the center of the foyer floor.

"What the hell is going on?" he muttered more to himself than anyone else.

Hearing a noise at the top of the stairs, he lifted his head to find Vanessa descending with Danny in her arms, two of his mother's staff trailing behind, arms loaded with even more of his ex-wife's and son's belongings.

"Thank you so much for all your help," Vanessa was saying. "I really appreciate it."

"What's going on?" he asked, more loudly this time.

Vanessa's head jerked up at his sharp tone or his sudden, unexpected appearance, or both.

"Marc," she breathed. "I wasn't expecting you back so soon."

"Obviously."

His brows drew down in an angry, suspicious frown as she stopped at the bottom of the steps. The two maids dipped their heads and mumbled about taking her things out to the waiting cab, then disappeared as quickly as they could.

"Sneaking off again?" he accused, not caring that his voice was cold with disappointment and betrayal.

She was leaving him again, was all he could think. He'd asked her to spend just a few days with his family—a week at the most—and she hadn't made it even two days.

They'd made love last night, more than once. Slept wrapped in each others' arms. He'd thought—stupidly, it turned out—that they had turned a corner and might actually be able to make their relationship work.

But while he'd been falling in love with her all over again and thinking about reconciliation, she'd been planning a timely escape. Exactly the same as before.

Exactly. Because the last time she'd left him, she'd been pregnant with his child…and there was a good chance the same was true now.

"No," Vanessa said, nervously licking her lips. "I mean, yes, I'm leaving, but no, I'm not trying to sneak off. I left you a note upstairs…on the back of the one you left for me this morning."

Well, that was different, at least, he thought with a heavy dose of sarcasm.

"And a note makes up for taking off in the middle of the day while I'm at the office?" he shot back. "With my son?"

"Of course not," she returned, looking strangely not guilty. "Although when you read the note, you'll see that I explained I'm not really taking off. I'm simply leaving the estate for a hotel downtown. I was going to stay there until I had the chance to talk to you."

He cocked his head, wondering what she could be up to. But then curiosity won out and he heard himself ask, "About what?"

She swallowed hard, her blue eyes going dark and oddly blank. "Your mother asked me to leave."

His own eyes went wide in surprise. "Why?" Why would his mother ask his wife—his ex-wife, he corrected himself silently—to leave?

"For the same reason she drove me away last time— because she hates me. Or at the very least disapproves of me greatly. As far as she's concerned, I'm not good enough for you and I never will be." A small smile touched her lips as she added, "Of course, this time she was much more forthright about wanting me gone, probably because I told her off."

"You told my mother off," he murmured, trying to process what he was hearing, but growing more confused by the minute. "Why would you do that?"

The amusement that had begun to touch Vanessa's features vanished, turning her face hard and defensive.

"Because I refuse to let her push me around any longer. I refuse to let her make me feel inferior just because *she* will always think of me as a lowly waitress, unworthy of her son's misguided affections."

Marc shook his head and started forward. "This is just a misunderstanding. Mother can be distant, I know, but she's thrilled about Danny and I'm sure she's pleased to have you back at the house, as well."

He reached out to grasp her shoulders, but she took a quick, single step back.

"No. It's not a misunderstanding, Marc," she told him, her tone implacable. "I know you love your mother and I would never ask you to change that. I would never intentionally try to drive a wedge between you and your family. But as much as I love you, I can't be here anymore."

Marc's chest tightened at her words. She loved him…or claimed to, at any rate yet she was preparing to walk away and leave him. Again.

"You love me," he scoffed, tossing the declaration back in her face. "Right. You love me, but you're leaving. Again. And what about Danny? What about the child you might be carrying now? My child. Are you going to run off and hide another pregnancy from me? Keep another baby from its father?"

She blanched at that, and God help him, he was glad. He knew he was being cruel, saying things to intentionally hurt her. But damn it, he was hurting, too. He was being betrayed a second time by the only woman he'd ever loved and who'd claimed—more than once—to love him in return.

"That's not fair, Marc," she said in a small voice, tightening her grip on Danny.

"The truth hurts, doesn't it, Vanessa? Signed divorce papers or no signed divorce papers, you knew you were pregnant when you left town the last time and you didn't even bother to tell me."

Because Danny was starting to fuss at her hip, she lowered her voice, but her temper came through loud and clear.

"Don't you dare lay that entirely at my feet. I kept Danny a secret, yes, but only after you refused to speak to me. I tried to tell you I was pregnant, but you couldn't be bothered to listen."

Marc's gaze narrowed. What game was she playing at now? he wondered. If what she said was true, it was news to him—and he sincerely believed he would remember his ex-wife telling him she was carrying his child.

"What are you talking about?" he asked carefully.

"I called you. As soon as I realized I was pregnant, I called you at the office, but you said—and I quote, because I will never forget the words as long as I live—*there's nothing you could possibly have to say to me that I want to hear.* End quote."

Well, now he knew something fishy was going on. Because he'd never uttered those words, not where Vanessa was concerned.

"I never said that," he murmured quietly.

"Yes," Vanessa retorted with conviction, "you did. Or at least that's the message Trevor said he was ordered to give me on your behalf."

"Trevor." It was a statement, not a question.

"Yes."

For a second, Marc wasn't certain if the thin sheen of crimson falling over his eyes was imaginary or if he was literally seeing red. He did know, however, that his blood pressure was rising like a geyser about to erupt and his hands were fisting with the urge to punch something. Or someone.

Reaching into his jacket pocket, he pulled out his cell phone and punched the button for his assistant's line at Keller Corp. Trevor Storch picked up on the first ring.

"Yes, sir," the overeager young man answered, well aware of who was calling thanks to Caller I.D.

"I'm out at the house. I want you here in under fifteen minutes."

"Yes, sir," Trevor responded dutifully and Marc could

almost see him jumping up and rounding his desk before he'd even returned the telephone to its cradle.

Meeting Vanessa's wary blue gaze, he snapped his own phone closed. "He'll be here soon and then we'll get to the bottom of this mess once and for all."

Fifteen

The seconds dragged on like hours, the minutes like years. Vanessa stood at the bottom of the stairs while the stony silence in the foyer grew heavier and more suffocating.

Danny wasn't getting any lighter, either. Shifting him to her other hip, she started to lower herself into a sitting position on one of the wide, carpeted steps, but Marc moved forward to stop her.

"Let me take him," he said brusquely, holding out his arms.

For a moment, she hesitated, the panicked thought that if she let Marc take the baby, she might never get him back racing through her mind. But if she tried to hold on to him now, then her avowals that she wouldn't try to keep Marc from seeing their son would be a lie, wouldn't they?

Hoping Marc hadn't noticed her uncertainty, she handed Danny over, rolling her shoulders and stretching her arms to work out the kinks.

"He's getting big, isn't he?" Marc said, a small smile curving his lips. The first he'd offered since spotting her luggage in the middle of the entryway.

"Yes, he is."

She was about to suggest they move into one of the nearby parlors to await Trevor's arrival, but just then a squeal of brakes came from the front drive and a minute later the door swung open.

Trevor Storch was tall, thin and more gangly than athletic. He stood just inside the foyer, brown hair mussed, shoulders sloped and breathing hard, as though he'd run most of the way from Keller Corp's main office building instead of driving.

Before he could say anything or begin bowing, as was his usual custom, Marc handed Danny back to her and turned on his assistant, any sign of kindness or amusement wiped from his face. Watching him close in on the younger man, even Vanessa had the urge to shy away and cover the baby's face to protect him from the steam that was almost literally pouring from Marc's ears.

Raising a hand practically in Trevor's face, Marc said in a low voice, "I'm going to ask you some questions and I want honest answers. God help you if you lie to me, do you understand?"

Any hint of eager anticipation drained from Storch's face, along with every bit of his skin's natural color. No doubt he'd thought he was being summoned to Keller Manor to run some extra-special errand or to receive a much-deserved—in his mind, at least—promotion.

"Y-yes, sir," he stammered, struggling to regain his composure.

"Did Vanessa call the office last year, just after we were divorced, and ask to speak with me?"

Trevor's eyes darted past Marc's shoulder to where she was standing, rocking slightly with the baby, who was currently content with attempting to fit his entire fist into his wide-open mouth.

"Yes or no, Trevor?" Marc demanded sharply.

"Y-yes, sir," he said, returning his attention to his very unhappy employer. "I believe she might have."

"And did you or did you not tell her that there was nothing she had to say to me that I wished to hear?"

At that, Trevor Storch's eyes went as wide as golf balls and his jaw dropped like a boulder. "I...I..."

He closed his mouth, licked his lips nervously. Then he seemed to deflate, his shoulders sinking even lower beneath his black shirt and beige sweater-vest than before.

"Yes, sir," he replied obediently, "I did."

Even from her vantage point near the stairwell, she saw Marc's brows dart upward in astonishment. Until that moment, she knew he hadn't believed her. He'd thought she was lying, or at the very least had suspected she was reinventing history to suit her purposes.

"Why?" he asked, shock and confusion evident in his tone.

"I...I..." Trevor's mouth open and closed like a guppy's and the color returned to his face in two rosy spots of nervous embarrassment.

"Because I told him to."

Eleanor's voice, deep and stern and coming out of nowhere, made Vanessa jump. Danny jerked in her arms at the sudden movement and began to fuss. She bounced up and down and pressed a kiss to the top of his head to shush him, but the greater part of her attention was on her ex-mother-in-law and the bomb she had just dropped into the middle of the cavernous foyer.

"Mother," Marc murmured, turning in her direction. "What are you talking about?"

Eleanor stepped from the doorway of the very same parlor

Vanessa had almost suggested they move to before Trevor's arrival, the heels of her powder blue pumps clicking regally on the thick parquet tiles.

"After your separation, I instructed Mr. Storch to field any calls that came into the office from Ms. Mason and to inform her that you didn't wish to speak to her again, for any reason."

Marc swung his disbelieving gaze from his mother to Travis and back again. Vanessa's own heart was pounding in her chest, emotion clogging her throat until it threatened to cut off her supply of oxygen.

All this time, she'd been so angry at Marc. So hurt that he could cut her off the way he had, that he could be so cruel and uncaring with a woman he'd once claimed to love…and who was unexpectedly carrying his child.

She knew, too, that Marc had probably been equally as angry and hurt at what he perceived to be her actions after they split, if he'd been expecting her to stay in at least moderate contact, only to have all of her calls impeded by his personal assistant.

Now she realized they had both been deceived.

"But…why?" Marc asked.

Eleanor's lips thinned. "She's trash, Marcus. Bad enough that you married her and brought her home in the first place. Having her continue to contact you and hang around after you finally wised up enough to divorce her would have been beyond unacceptable. As though I would ever stand by and allow her to work her wiles and trick you into taking her back."

"So you ordered *my* assistant to block *my wife's* attempts to contact me." It was a statement, not a question.

Eleanor had known Marc all his life, while Vanessa had known him for only a handful of years. Yet his mother seemed ignorant of the resentment building in the heat of his green eyes and the clenching of his fists at his sides.

"Of course," Eleanor responded haughtily, tipping her nose another few centimeters into the air. "I would do anything to protect the Keller name from gold diggers like her."

"Her name," Marc intoned from between gritted teeth, "is Vanessa."

Before his mother could respond to that bit of information, he crossed to Vanessa and plucked Danny right out of her arms. While she floundered, unsure of what to think or do, he grabbed her elbow, ran his hand the rest of the way down her arm and threaded his fingers with hers. He marched them past the pile of her packed belongings nearly to the door, stopping a mere foot from Trevor's trembling form.

"You're fired," he told the young man in a brook-no-arguments tone. "Return to the office, clear out your desk and leave. You're welcome to work for my mother, if she'll have you, since the two of you certainly deserve each other, but I don't want to see you anywhere near Keller Corp ever again. Is that understood?"

Vanessa could have sworn she saw tears fill Trevor's eyes just before he ducked his head to stare at the tops of his shoes. "Yes, sir," he said in a watery voice.

"And you," Marc continued, turning this time to glare at his mother. "I always thought Vanessa was exaggerating when she told me how badly you were behaving toward her behind my back, because I didn't want to believe my own mother would treat the woman I loved as anything other than a true member of this family. But she was right all along, wasn't she?"

Marc paused for a moment, but Vanessa didn't think it was to allow Eleanor to respond. "You won't see us again. Not here. I'll send for my belongings and anything Vanessa might have left behind. But the company is mine. Mine and Adam's.

You're off the Board of Directors as of now and your name will be removed from anything related to the corporation."

Eleanor's nostrils flared as she sucked in a breath, and Vanessa saw the first shadow of fear cross her severe features.

"You can't do that," she rasped.

Marc's gaze narrowed, his expression every bit as unyielding as his mother's at that moment. "Watch me."

With that, he yanked open the front door and stalked through, tugging Vanessa along behind him. The two servants who had been helping her carry her things to the waiting taxi were standing beside the bright yellow car, doing their best to remain inconspicuous and out of what she was sure they assumed would be the line of fire.

"Put all of Vanessa's things in my car," he told them, transferring Danny back to her. The poor baby was probably beginning to feel like a racquetball, though from his happy gurgles, he seemed to think being passed from one parent to the other and back again was some sort of game.

Then Marc crossed to the cab and leaned in the open window to speak in low tones to the man behind the wheel. After Marc slipped him a few folded-up bills, the driver nodded, and Marc returned to her side.

"What are we doing?" she asked, still unable to believe all that had just happened.

Lifting a hand to cup her face, he said, "We're leaving. We'll stay at a hotel until I can get things straightened out at the office, then we'll head back to Summerville."

"But…"

"No buts." He shook his head, his gaze immediately softening to a lovely emerald green. "I'm so sorry, Vanessa. I didn't see it. I didn't believe you because I didn't want to admit my family was anything but perfect, that one of them would treat my wife with anything but love and respect."

His thumb rubbed slowly back and forth across her cheek, and she felt herself melting.

"If I had known, if I had truly understood what you were going through, I would have stopped it. I never would have let things between us turn out the way they did."

Her throat was so tight, she couldn't speak, but she believed him. After what he'd just done, how he'd stood up to his mother and walked away from his family home *for her,* how could she not?

"I love you, Vanessa. I've always loved you and I'm so sorry for all the time I've wasted being a blind, stupid fool."

She sniffed as happy tears filled her eyes and balanced precariously on the tips of her lashes.

He leaned in, pressing his brow to hers, and said barely above a whisper, "If I could go back and do things differently, I would never let you go."

A near-sob rolled up from her chest, causing those tears to spill over and roll down her cheeks.

"I love you, too," she told him. "And I never wanted to leave, I just couldn't live that way anymore."

"I know that," he said with more understanding than she'd heard from him in longer than she could remember.

"And I didn't plan to keep Danny a secret from you. I really did try to tell you, but after Trevor refused to let me speak to you, I was so angry and hurt, thinking the directive came from you…" She trailed off, barely certain anymore of how she'd felt or what had led her to make the decisions she had.

"I know," Marc murmured, one corner of his mouth lifting in a kind, loving half smile. He looked at their son with a father's love and pride burning in his eyes before brushing a hand over the baby's downy-soft head.

"We both made mistakes and let small issues become big ones. But we won't let that happen again, will we?"

She shook her head, doing her best to blink back fresh tears.

Framing her face with his big, strong hands, he brushed his lips lightly across hers. "I really do love you, Nessa. Forever."

"I love you, too," she tried to say, but his mouth was already covering hers, kissing her deeply, with all the passion that had bloomed between them since the first moment they'd met.

Epilogue

Two years later...

Marc strolled down the sidewalk of Summerville's Main Street, nodding and waving a greeting to friends as he passed. And he was whistling, for heaven's sake. He never used to whistle, but lately, he'd caught himself doing it more and more often.

Which just went to prove that small town life wasn't quite as dull or restrictive as he'd once believed. In fact, he kind of liked it.

Of course, he didn't think his current happiness had as much to do with where he was living as it did with *how* he was living...and with whom.

Hiking Danny higher on his hip, he continued to whistle— the theme from *Thomas the Tank Engine*, no less—and grinned at his son's hearty chuckle. He was wearing a pair of denim trousers with an official Sugar Shack infant tee and tiny yellow sneakers.

The Sugar Shack merchandise had been Marc's idea and had been an immediate success. In addition to baked goods, they now sold T-shirts, sweatshirts, baby clothes, coffee and travel mugs, and even key chains. In his opinion, it was the best advertising Vanessa could get other than plain old word of mouth.

The sneakers were because Danny was walking now…well, toddling, was more like it…and because he was starting to want to dress more like his daddy. Marc's heart gave a lurch at the thought and he squeezed his son even tighter against his side.

"We're going to see Mommy," he told the little boy, then added, "Maybe she'll give you a cookie."

"Cookie!" Danny yelled at the top of his lungs, lifting his arms and clapping over his head.

Marc laughed, wondering how much trouble he would get in when Vanessa found out he was plying their son with promises of sugar first thing in the morning. But then, she ran a bakery, so she shouldn't be surprised. "Cookie" had been Danny's first word…followed by "mama," "dada" and "cake." He was working on "baklava," but at the moment it came out more like "bababa."

Reaching The Sugar Shack's wide glass storefront, he pulled open the door to the distribution side of the business. An elderly woman was just shuffling out, so he held it for her and wished her a good day before slipping inside.

Vanessa was behind the counter, but as soon as she saw them, she smiled and started around. Her copper curls— longer now than when Danny had been an infant—were pulled back in a loose ponytail, and a pristine white Sugar Shack apron covered the front of her short-sleeve blouse and shorts.

"Cookie!" Danny cried, wiggling to be put down.

Vanessa arched a brow. "His idea, I'm sure," she murmured half under her breath.

"Of course," Marc replied. "But then, what can you expect when his mother owns the best bakery in the state? You're lucky he isn't asking for pastries morning, noon and night."

"He is, but that doesn't mean he'll get them," she answered primly.

Leaning in, she bussed Danny on the cheek, running her fingers through his toffee-brown hair, which was rather in need of a trim. They'd been talking lately about having it cut and Marc was inordinately excited about taking his son for his first visit to the barber shop. An honest-to-goodness barber shop!

When she lifted up on tiptoe to kiss him, too, he slipped his free arm around her back and pulled her in for something much longer and deeper. Trapped between them, Danny giggled when they stayed locked at the lips a bit too long and started slapping their cheeks with his small hands.

They pulled apart, and Vanessa chuckled, her face flushing a becoming shade of pink. Marc, however, was far from embarrassed; he was busy calculating how many hours were left before she closed up shop and he could convince her to go to bed early.

Too damn many, that was for sure.

"I have a surprise for you," he told her as she moved back behind the counter.

He watched her loosen the ties of her apron and slip it over her head, then dig inside a small plastic container that she kept filled with cookies just for Danny. Their son's love of sweets had prompted her to experiment with a few recipes for healthier cookies and desserts. Ones with less fat and sugar, and substitutions such as applesauce and raisin paste for the oils.

Coming around again, she handed Danny the cookie, and Marc set him on one of the high countertops to eat it, remaining close enough to keep him from toppling off.

Without the apron, Vanessa's four months of pregnancy were much more noticeable. And just like every time he saw that tiny baby bump, Marc's chest constricted with love and pride and the overwhelming relief of knowing that—even though they'd cut it damn close—he hadn't let her get away.

As much as they'd suspected it for a while, she hadn't been pregnant when they'd walked away from his family's home. Instead, they'd had some time to settle in Summerville and adjust to once again being together. Not that there had been a lot of adjustment needed, at least not on his part.

They'd bought a large, very nice house on the outskirts of town. One that had been built years before by a wealthy businessman who'd decided to move closer to the city after he and his wife divorced.

It was smaller than Marc was used to, but exceptionally large and impressive for the area. It also had plenty of room for their growing family, and came with enough acreage to afford complete privacy, as well as room for Danny and his future siblings to play.

They had also gotten remarried. At the courthouse this time, with a minimum of fuss and muss. Only Helen had been in attendance as their witness, as well as Vanessa's matron-of-honor and Danny's stand-in-nanny. He actually thought she might be coming around to liking him, but he knew he would have to prove himself all over again to be worthy of her niece's affections before he could truly win back the woman's favor.

After everything they'd been through, it had been easy to agree that another big wedding wasn't necessary. They just wanted to be together again, undoing the divorce that they both wished had never taken place in the first place.

Then they'd discussed having another child. One he would know about and be involved with from the very beginning.

"So," Vanessa prompted. "What's my surprise?" She tilted her head and shot him an impish grin, one he couldn't resist kissing off her lips.

Breaking away much sooner than he would have liked, he reached into the back pocket of his khaki chinos and pulled out a folded-over, full-color catalog. He let it fall open and held it up for her to see.

"Oh, my God!" She gave a squeal of pleasure and grabbed it up, studying the front and back covers first, then flipping through each individual page. "I can't believe it's finally ready. It's wonderful!"

It was The Sugar Shack's very first mail-order catalog, but Marc sincerely hoped it wouldn't be the last. Since leaving Pittsburgh, he'd thrown himself wholeheartedly into helping Vanessa build her business. He still drove into the city occasionally to take care of Keller Corp affairs, but was content to allow his brother to deal with the daily running of that company and the family's other major holdings.

In addition to designing the catalog, he'd set up a website for the bakery and was looking into rental spaces in other surrounding towns with an eye toward opening more Sugar Shack bakeries in multiple locations.

"I have more good news," he said while she continued to admire the pages of the catalog.

"What?" she asked, lifting her head and looking positively giddy.

He smiled in return, because he couldn't seem to help himself. "Adam and I finalized an agreement this morning to open a Sugar Shack bakery in the lobby of the Keller Corp building."

Marc expected her to shriek with joy and throw her arms

around her neck, but instead she grew quiet and simply studied him.

"What's the matter?" he asked, cocking his head in confusion. "I thought you would be happy about this."

She nodded. "I am. Everything you've done has been wonderful—more than Aunt Helen and I ever could have imagined."

"But...?"

Her mouth twisted, her eyes growing concerned. "But I worry about what your mother will think of you and Adam working together to put *my* business in the lobby of your family's company headquarters. And if we really do move back to the city one of these days the way we've discussed..."

She trailed off and he could see every one of her doubts playing across her face.

"She already knows," he told her.

Her mouth went slack with shock.

"According to Adam, she's asked about us several times, and he's been updating her. I don't want to get your hopes up—" he grinned as she rolled her eyes at the possibility "—but he seems to think she might be coming around."

Vanessa gave a disbelieving snort and he chuckled. "All right. So she'll never be the cookie-baking, story-telling sort of mother or grandmother we might wish she were, but I think walking away and cutting her out of our lives for a while showed her that I'm serious in my devotion to you. You're my wife and I won't allow anyone or anything to ever hurt you or come between us again. Not even the woman who gave birth to me."

Stepping forward, she rested her hands and then her head on his chest. "Are you sorry?" she murmured against his shirt.

Framing her face with his hands, he tipped her chin up and

met her storm blue gaze. "Not even a little bit. I don't ever want you to think that, okay? You and Danny—" he tipped his head toward their crumb-covered son "—and this tiny tyke here—" he pressed a hand flat to her growing belly "—are all that matter to me. I haven't closed the door on rebuilding a relationship with my mother, but I wouldn't trade my life now with the three of you for anything in the world. Do you understand?"

It took her a second, but she nodded slowly, and he stared into her eyes until he was sure she believed him.

"Good. Then I'll get our little Cookie Monster cleaned up while you go show your aunt the new catalog. Hopefully it will put her in a good enough mood that we can ask her to watch Danny for a while this afternoon."

"Why?" Vanessa asked.

His mouth spread in a wolfish grin and he leaned in to brush his lips across hers. "Because I'm in the mood for something sweet."

Cocking her head to the side, she narrowed her eyes, giving him a sultry, seductive look. "Well, this *is* a bakery. Sweets are what we're all about."

He gave a low growl at her wicked flirtation and nearly told her how lucky she was that Danny was with them and the bakery was fronted by floor-to-ceiling plate glass windows. Otherwise, he would be lifting her onto one of the countertops and divesting her of her clothes already.

"What I want isn't on the menu."

"So you have a special order?" she asked, batting those lashes until he felt his insides start to boil.

He nodded, mouth gone too dry to respond.

"Lucky for you, and thanks to my very business-savvy husband, we're set up to take special orders now. You may have to pay extra for shipping and handling, though."

Lips twitching, he said in a low voice, "That shouldn't be a problem. In case you haven't heard, I'm rich."

She smiled softly and reached up to wrap her arms around his neck. "So am I," she whispered.

And neither of them were talking about their bank accounts.

* * * * *

Harlequin® Desire

COMING NEXT MONTH

Available July 12, 2011

#2095 CAUGHT IN THE BILLIONAIRE'S EMBRACE
Elizabeth Bevarly

#2096 ONE NIGHT, TWO HEIRS
Maureen Child
Texas Cattleman's Club: The Showdown

#2097 THE TYCOON'S TEMPORARY BABY
Emily McKay
Billionaires and Babies

#2098 A LONE STAR LOVE AFFAIR
Sara Orwig
Stetsons & CEOs

#2099 ONE MONTH WITH THE MAGNATE
Michelle Celmer
Black Gold Billionaires

#2100 FALLING FOR THE PRINCESS
Sandra Hyatt

You can find more information on upcoming
Harlequin® titles, free excerpts and more at
www.HarlequinInsideRomance.com.

HDCNM0611

REQUEST YOUR FREE BOOKS!

2 FREE NOVELS PLUS 2 FREE GIFTS!

ALWAYS POWERFUL, PASSIONATE AND PROVOCATIVE

YES! Please send me 2 FREE Harlequin Desire® novels and my 2 FREE gifts (gifts are worth about $10). After receiving them, if I don't wish to receive any more books, I can return the shipping statement marked "cancel." If I don't cancel, I will receive 6 brand-new novels every month and be billed just $4.05 per book in the U.S. or $4.74 per book in Canada. That's a saving of at least 15% off the cover price! It's quite a bargain! Shipping and handling is just 50¢ per book in the U.S. and 75¢ per book in Canada.* I understand that accepting the 2 free books and gifts places me under no obligation to buy anything. I can always return a shipment and cancel at any time. Even if I never buy another book, the two free books and gifts are mine to keep forever.

225/326 SDN FC65

Name _____ (PLEASE PRINT) _____

Address _____ Apt. # _____

City _____ State/Prov. _____ Zip/Postal Code _____

Signature (if under 18, a parent or guardian must sign)

Mail to the **Reader Service:**
IN U.S.A.: P.O. Box 1867, Buffalo, NY 14240-1867
IN CANADA: P.O. Box 609, Fort Erie, Ontario L2A 5X3

Not valid for current subscribers to Harlequin Desire books.

Want to try two free books from another line?
Call 1-800-873-8635 or visit www.ReaderService.com.

* Terms and prices subject to change without notice. Prices do not include applicable taxes. Sales tax applicable in N.Y. Canadian residents will be charged applicable taxes. Offer not valid in Quebec. This offer is limited to one order per household. All orders subject to credit approval. Credit or debit balances in a customer's account(s) may be offset by any other outstanding balance owed by or to the customer. Please allow 4 to 6 weeks for delivery. Offer available while quantities last.

Your Privacy—The Reader Service is committed to protecting your privacy. Our Privacy Policy is available online at www.ReaderService.com or upon request from the Reader Service.

We make a portion of our mailing list available to reputable third parties that offer products we believe may interest you. If you prefer that we not exchange your name with third parties, or if you wish to clarify or modify your communication preferences, please visit us at www.ReaderService.com/consumerschoice or write to us at Reader Service Preference Service, P.O. Box 9062, Buffalo, NY 14269. Include your complete name and address.

USA TODAY *bestselling author B.J. Daniels*
takes you on a trip to Whitehorse, Montana,
and the Chisholm Cattle Company.

RUSTLED

Available July 2011 from Harlequin Intrigue.

As the dust settled, Dawson got his first good look at the rustler. A pair of big Montana sky-blue eyes glared up at him from a face framed by blond curls.

A woman rustler?

"You have to let me go," she hollered as the roar of the stampeding cattle died off in the distance.

"So you can finish stealing my cattle? I don't think so." Dawson jerked the woman to her feet.

She reached for the gun strapped to her hip hidden under her long barn jacket.

He grabbed the weapon before she could, his eyes narrowing as he assessed her. "How many others are there?" he demanded, grabbing a fistful of her jacket. "I think you'd better start talking before I tear into you."

She tried to fight him off, but he was on to her tricks and pinned her to the ground. He was suddenly aware of the soft curves beneath the jean jacket she wore under her coat.

"You have to listen to me." She ground out the words from between her gritted teeth. "You have to let me go. If you don't they will come back for me and they will kill you. There are too many of them for you to fight off alone. You won't stand a chance and I don't want your blood on my hands."

"I'm touched by your concern for me. Especially after you just tried to pull a gun on me."

"I wasn't going to shoot you."

Dawson hauled her to her feet and walked her the rest of the way to his horse. Reaching into his saddlebag, he pulled out a length of rope.

"You can't tie me up."

He pulled her hands behind her back and began to tie her wrists together.

"If you let me go, I can keep them from coming back," she said. "You have my word." She let out an unladylike curse. "I'm just trying to save your sorry neck."

"And I'm just going after my cattle."

"Don't you mean your boss's cattle?"

"Those cattle are mine."

"*You're* a Chisholm?"

"Dawson Chisholm. And you are…?"

"Everyone calls me Jinx."

He chuckled. "I can see why."

Bronco busting, falling in love…it's all in a day's work.
Look for the rest of their story in

RUSTLED

Available July 2011 from Harlequin Intrigue
wherever books are sold.

THE NOTORIOUS
WOLFES

**A powerful dynasty,
where secrets and scandal never sleep!**

Eight siblings, blessed with wealth, but denied the one
thing they wanted—a father's love. Haunted by their
past and driven to succeed, the Wolfes scattered to the
far corners of the globe. It's said that even the blackest
of souls can be healed by the purest of love....

But can the dynasty rise again?

Beginning July 2011

8 volumes to collect and treasure!